GLORY
THE CANNON FODDER SERIES BOOK 3

Andrew C. Suhrer

ISBN: 8218130268
ISBN-13: 979-8218130268

Glory - The Cannon Fodder Series Book 3

Copyright © 2022 by Andrew C. Suhrer

Cover Design: David London of London Studios
Editing & Layout by: Dequiana Jackson of Inspired Marketing, Inc.

PROLOGUE

CALVIN opened his eyes and found himself naked on a soft bed. His body was numb and exposed to the air with bed sheets pushed off the mattress. He could see a light show above in the state room that made it look like he was flying through the stars. His eyes slowly adjusted to the darkness. He felt something he had not felt in some time and that was intoxication. Calvin figured it was caused by the empty liquor bottles, syringes, and pill bottles strung out across the deck. He rolled over and saw Holly next to him sleeping in the open. Calvin could not help but go wide eyed at the sight of her. She was stunning. Her skin was smooth as silk and her body had curves giving her an hourglass figure. The last thing he remembered was vandalizing the classroom he was in. Despite the surprise, he didn't panic as this was the best wake-up-call he could think of. He wasn't at risk of immediate danger for once. He couldn't help but smirk a little, thrilled that he'd gotten laid despite knowing he was just being used. Holly woke up and put an arm over Calvin's chest. She laughed as she leaned up towards him moving her black hair from her face showing her smile, "Leaving so soon?"

"Huh… must I?" he asked in confusion as the intoxicants still affected him. She pulled his face towards her and kissed him. A mix of the booze and the affection caused him to get swept away. He reached up, caressing her cheek as they made out. Calvin's eyes went wide again as he saw a former lover in front of him instead of Holly. The hair was now red, and the blue eyes were now green. It was either the hallucination or Holly saying to him, "Don't worry. You're just going crazy from all the abuse you've been through."

"That's reassuring," he jokingly replied before she kissed him again and rolled on top of him. Calvin allowed it, wanting to feel the warmth and comfort of another. His fears about the future vanished as their lips pressed together, something that he'd been denied for too long. In his arousal, Holly lowered herself on top of him. She laughed, "So much better now that you're more coherent!"

"I improve with every action." He smiled while she started moving. Again, he saw his former lover on top of him instead of Holly in the flashes of light. Setting aside guilt, shame, and remorse, he pushed up into her making her gasp. Her moans got louder as he lifted himself off the mattress. She was almost touching the overhead with each upward push. A voice came on the intercom and the lights flashed from the holographic projection, "Admiral, we arrived at... is now a bad time?"

"This is a good time! Enjoying the show?" she shouted while still moving herself up and down without missing a beat. Calvin was in shock at how she was multitasking so well. He didn't know what to put his focus on as she kept going in front of the subordinate. The Petty Officer stuttered, "Ma'am... with respect, you made it loud and clear that..."

"Run the damned message to my quarters! Shit!" She shouted while gyrating her hips. Calvin gasped as she kept the motion ignoring the audience they had. He let out a gasp as he saw a holographic screen of an alien pop up in front of him. "May I help you with something?"

"May you? You're supposed to. I let you fucks live. Time to deliver on your end of the bargain. Also, I thought your race had hang ups about openly fornicating over a communication link." The alien code named "Claw" appeared above them. Her given name was Irene. Holly snapped at her despite the reptile looking like something out of nightmares. Irene had four thin red eyes, a wide shark smile with jagged teeth and scaled skin. "Do

2

you want me to…"

"Hang ups are for the losers of the past! Not to mention we weren't the ones who came up with a shitty false flag that blew up in your face! Now we just arrived at our home system and we're about to get the Dragon's Teeth up and running! Unlike your poorly conceived conniving, this plan isn't going to backfire on me!" Holly snapped as she slammed her body down on top of Calvin's. He somehow managed to stay stiff despite the unwelcome guest. Holly kept him stimulated with her embrace. She was letting go of formality and allowing herself to smile as Irene scoffed, "You're relying way too much on luck and miracles. Are you all going to keep that up while…?"

"Now who's the one with hang ups? You seem to trust in our fortune, seeing how we're working together again! If you just took your time and connived your way to the top instead of getting impatient, your faction wouldn't be on the ropes by the Valkyries right now! Never put the home world at risk moron!" She shouted at her while increasing her speed of movement. Irene grumbled, "We won't be for long, and they'll be coming for you all soon enough. Remember that."

The communication link went off as Holly laughed. "Finally! She's as clueless as she is annoying! So glad I didn't have to climax to that! Speaking of…"

Calvin's mouth dropped open as she went up and down like a jack hammer. He let out a long gasp right when they both felt a climax. She dropped on top of him shaking and dragging her nails across his chest. They were both still twitching as they cooled off. She looked up at him, "No gratitude? If it weren't for me, you wouldn't be enjoying that two by four you have now."

He gave a sheepish smile in begrudging agreement seemingly okay with the results. She jabbed him with a needle and his haze was gone. He was sober in seconds. She rolled off him sighing, "While we've got time, I'm curious on what drives you…besides avoiding getting

3

killed."

"Huh?" Calvin asked her in confusion once again. She sighed, "Why are you fighting?"

"Like you said, I like to not die," he told her honestly as she smiled, "Just that? Not wondering why you follow orders or play along? You didn't seem to have the balls to do what was necessary earlier."

"I have priorities. Wait. What are you getting at? Really going to bring up that forced augmentation again?" Calvin quick regretted bringing that subject up as he sat up, stretching himself out. Holly grabbed his face to look at her, "I wanted to see if you'd do anything to win. Now I know you won't. Kind of disappointed. Then again, you always seemed to be the more submissive type."

"You might be great in bed Holly, but you're still a condescending psycho bitch," he told her bluntly without fear of reprisal. Oddly, this made her laugh, "Yet, you still obey like a good boy. Call my methods dirty, but they got results."

"Your amoral attitude aside; how did you get those results? Honestly think you're a witch for convincing aliens that we're just fighting to not kill us and then allow us to work with them again." Calvin told her finally able to process everything he'd just endured. She replied, "Life cheated us, so I cheated at life. What do you want now that you survived the impossible?"

"Well, I…" Calvin thought about it for a few seconds and the only things that popped to mind he'd already gotten: fighting, drinking and fornication. There was one more thought that came to mind, but he didn't want to share it with her. Shrugging he replied, "Do what we did last night again."

"Figured you'd come back for more. I'd love to do another round now, but duty calls. I look forward to seeing what you can do while not spiked up."

"Wait. You drugged me?" He asked her already knowing the answer to the question. Calvin was once more reminded that he was just being used. Holly hopped off the bed and walked over to a workstation. She pulled up holographic images of the Sol system. "Don't worry love. Still did your job. You'll be seeing Marley, Jr. soon enough. Maybe more with how well you work."

"Wait, Junior? More ways? What?" He asked her, standing up with soreness suddenly setting in. His body felt like it ran a marathon. "I'd tell you to be a better father than you were the last two times, but we both know that's not going to be the case. Hopefully, Hail likes you more than Yeager and Vera did or could."

"Hail? Wait, what do you know?" He asked her still shocked and confused. She smiled, "A lot of things. Hail sounded like a good name as any. I had inspiration for that name from my father."

She paused for a moment when she saw footage being fed into her monitor. For a brief second, she looked concerned. Quickly going back to her cold self, she turned off the monitor before Calvin could see what she was looking at. "At least you'll be looking for a needle in an empty barn."

"Okay, this coy shit is getting really old," Calvin grumbled knowing he was being lead on again. She smirked, "This timeline's downfall is our rise. Try relaxing. After this mission, everything you'll do is all voluntary. Now kindly get out."

"Fine," he sighed grabbing his clothing. As he was about to get dressed the door opened and Holly pulled out a side arm, "Want to risk resurrection while it's still under repair?"

"Psycho," he scoffed while heading for the door. As it closed Holly laughed, "You know you like it!"

Calvin was left in the passageway exposed as others passed by laughing, "Way to climb the chain of command there, boy toy!"

"Did she at least give you knee pads?" Another person said.

"Had to earn your rank the hard way?"

"Redefining sucking up!"

He stood there looking at the door in disbelief at his situation and slightly embarrassed. Calvin grumbled to himself, "The more things change, the more they stay the same."

CHAPTER 1
CLEAN
DATE CURRENTLY UNKNOWN
C.S.W. (CONSORTIUM SHIP OF WAR) JASON
BERTHING

CALVIN wandered around the ship not bothering to put on his clothes as he figured his shame was complete and couldn't sink any lower. All around him the ship was being repaired. He was still amazed at what she endured and at what everyone survived. There were other festivities going on with groups of personnel chanting in celebration, "We're not dead!"

Partying was one way to deal with all the loss, pain and suffering that they just experienced. He tried not think about it, but the memories hung over him like an anvil. Them returning to the home system didn't help as those that damned him to that mission were there. He managed to figure out where the Chief's berthing was and walked inside. It was much nicer than the regular enlisted berth with more room, amenities, and some larger racks. Lane and Rotten were both inside already. The curtain was drawn on their rack. They were going at it, making loud noises as they bumped into each other. Calvin let them be as he went into the showers. He quickly went to the closest shower head and let the water pour over him, cleaning himself off. He was thankful the ship's gravity and plumbing was working again. The ship showed signs of wear and tear with all the patch work that had been done to replace all the damage. With what had occurred, it was a miracle she was still flying. Calvin changed his thoughts, not wanting to think about facing his mortality once more, sending a shiver down his spine. Dying once was bad, but multiple times was agonizing. The hot water helped calm him down as he groaned, releasing all his pent-up anxiety. He realized that this was the first break he'd had in some time. The thoughts kept coming as he leaned against the metal bulkhead gasping. Dread started to set in as he knew it wasn't over yet. There was more to come. At least for now, he felt safe. Still the thoughts crept into his head about what Holly just asked him, "Why am I doing this?"

He opened his eyes again when Valery stumbled into the bathroom naked with a bottle of liquor and a bottle of pills saying, "Stop being such a bitch! We're not dead, fucker!"

"Uh… no. No, we're not," he replied as she fell down next to him in the shower laughing, "Want some?"

"I'm good. Had my share earlier," he quickly told her. She laughed at him, "Oh? How was it with Holly? She looks like a witch!"

"Word gets around quickly doesn't it," he lamented as he clinched his lips together in embarrassment. Valery looked up at him, "You just did the walk of shame from her stateroom. Painfully obvious on how you're earning your rank."

She gave him a wink. He grumbled. "You're just envious that you couldn't earn yours like that," he told her jokingly as she took a swig of her drink, "One day I will!"

"Don't be in any rush," he told her as she downed some more pills. "Don't be a buzz kill. We're not actively having to fight for our lives for once. We just got laid and now we're getting high as a kite!"

"Laid?" He asked her, wondering who she was with and whether what he just did was legitimate. Valery laughed, "Well, as for your case, sounds like molestation."

"Oh, fuck off," he grumbled back at her defensively. She laughed harder, "You got used as a fuck toy!"

"Shut up! Oh, what the hell. I'll take some pills," Calvin said to her, changing his mind. She purposely put them all in her mouth giggling, "Had your chance!"

"Says you!" In desperation to feel something other than humiliation and despite being denied the pills, he leaned forward, shoving his tongue into her mouth trying to get the pills. Valery both laughed and squealed at the same time, as Calvin ended up on top of her. Swallowing several of the capsules, he looked down at her as the drugs kicked in. As the intoxicants ran through his system, all morality went out the window. Calvin sighed, "Why not?"

As he pushed down into Valery, she gasped, "We're sort of the same person…"

"Who cares?" He told her as he thrusted downwards. "Oh fuck!"

Calvin laughed as their bodies became heated from the scalding hot water and the intoxicants flowing through them. Calvin laughed, "Morality is for chumps!"

"You've been hanging out with Holly too long!" She snapped back at him as her eyes rolled into the back of her head, "Finish up! I'm burning up!"

He moved his body rapidly with the enhancements. Valery was leaving several scratch marks on the tails as they both reached their climax. Calvin slowed down his movements as they gasped. After a couple minutes of silence Valery grumbled, "We're fucking terrible degenerates. Why did we do that?"

"Now who's being the downer? Are the pills making you bipolar?" He spoke with a tired voice. He sat back up just wanting to get clean as he started rubbing the soap into his skin. Valery looked at him, "Not thinking about it?"

"Dealing with existentialism. Yet again, I just

committed masturbation and I don't care," he told her as she huffed, "You sound like a drone. Not thinking about things and blindly following orders haven't exactly been working out for us."

"We're not dead so we're doing something right," Calvin pointed out as he kept rubbing himself still not feeling clean. A loud bang sent him into shock, causing him to drop the soap. Valery laughed, "Know what they say about dropping the soap in the shower."

She took the now empty bottle and shoved it into two of her fingers, forming a circle and made a facial expression of pain and shock. Calvin started laughing, "Not going to get me a drink first?"

"You took my pills!" She pointed at him jokingly. Calvin sighted, "Butt chugging booze is too much of a pain in the ass."

Valery laughed, "You perverted bastard!"

Calvin kicked the bar of soap against the bulkhead and coughed, "I'm the damned top this time!"

"Too bad that wasn't the case with your girlfriend," Valery mentioned trying to mess with him. Calvin huffed, "Unless you want to do another round, stop talking about the witch. Okay?"

"Wow... we really are degenerates. Never mind. So why didn't you get dressed?" she asked wanting to change the subject.

"It was too late. Plus, why bother if I was just going to strip again anyway?" He told her, trying to hide his discomfort, "I got bigger problems than being used."

"Being used causes all your problems. You honestly thought you were another person there for a while. Never occurred to you to ask anything until it was too late." Valery bluntly pointed out his past mistakes. Calvin grumbled, "I didn't know shit about what the hell was going on. No past, no guidance for the future. Okay? Good news... I think. Got another kid on the way apparently. Hopefully, this one doesn't throw me under the bus."

Valery correctly speculated what he was talking about, "Guessing you're referring to Yeager. Well at least there should be Vera, right?"

"How did you..." He started asking her as she smiled at him, "You talk in your sleep like all the fucking time, lunatic."

"Damn. How the hell did I end up a broken record?" Calvin wondered aloud. Thinking about it reminded him of why he sunk to such low levels of depravity: to feel something other than helplessness. "Lighten up! Every record is going to have its scratches. After all the bullshit we've been through, I think we have the right to gripe a little. Don't let anyone call you a cry baby! But you are being a cry baby," said Valery.

"So says the whiner. Save the psychiatry for when you're sober. Then you can make a profit off daddy issues," Calvin told her jokingly.

"Shrink? I was thinking of being an artist who took cat photos," Valery told him trying to change the subject again. Calvin laughed, "Cats huh? I think there was a phrase called Furry. Was that your...?"

"No, you bastard! I might be guilty of benefiting from horrible crimes, degeneracy and drug use, but not that!" She grumbled looking at the empty pill bottle. Calvin just cut to the chase, "So we got lied to, killed a bunch of innocent people, died multiple times horribly, got molested, survived a zombie apocalypse, and now we just committed selfcest. Who hasn't made a few mistakes in their life?"

"Don't think about the dead. They wouldn't think about us," she told him while hitting the glass bottle on the blue tiles. "That bitch is breaking us apart."

"What do you mean?"

Valery explained, "Have you looked around recently? Not many of us are left after that epic cluster fuck back in the Claw system. Claw? What kind of name is that?

Well, no dumber than Stallion. Aliens are strange. Well, Holly is making us squad leaders. That means we're going to see less of each other."

"Oh damn," he grumbled in dismay, not wanting to lose the closest person that he had as a friend. Valery paused smiling, "You like me!"

"Yeah…" He admitted as she laughed. Once she was done, she looked down sighing, "Don't you ever use protection?"

"Just when in combat… oh." He realized the implications of what he did as Valery sighed, "Shit. Heard masturbation creates clones. Oh, we suck…"

She stopped and they both were silent as the showers kept running. Valery changed the subject, "So…what do you think became of Yeager and Vera? Didn't one of them turn on you?"

Calvin struggled to not snap at her for her crass words. "We just talked about this. Your guess is good as mine. This is another time, so anything is possible. Looks like civilization took a hit after the Valkyrie weapon struck the home system."

"Yeah. Almost forgot about that bit. Easy to take over when there's only ashes remaining," Valery mentioned while playing with the bottle still. Calvin sighed, "Trippy, isn't it? Like everything we did, got expunged in an instant."

"Nothing we did mattered?" Valery asked him with a hint of annoyance in her voice. Calvin quickly told her, "Matters to us for what it's worth."

"It's something, I guess. Think this Consortium is just as bad as the Alliance or Spartans? Spartan named totally got overused!" She now drank the water that filled her bottle, not being able to tell the difference.

"Though we're going by Mongols," Calvin commented, taking a seat. Valery told him, "Mongols is the name of the first Special Operations Division, one of many. I think they're here to make sure we don't fail.

Those motherfuckers are over eight feet tall and seem like they're roid raging! Guess that means we're back to being meat shields. As for the overall organization, it's going by Consortium. Got it?"

"For being intoxicated, you're well informed. Going by a height index for superiority? Never mind. Holly mentioned something about one more mission before things become voluntary. Know something I don't?" He asked her. Valery looked up at him, "She must be screwing with us."

"More than likely. Wait, does Deus Ex Machina work in this timeline? Seems too good to be true." Calvin thought about their unnatural abilities. Valery looked up, "If it is too good to be true, it's not. What is good and true is the time we got. Want to go again?"

Calvin looked down at her as she presented herself to him. He sighed, "Why not?"

Chapter 2
Returning
Date Unknown
Sol System
C.W.S Jason
Chief Petty Officer's Berthing

CALVIN was puzzled by the dark blue coveralls that he now had to wear. Besides pockets, the only other distinguishing feature was the patch that had his rank, name, and a Titan's head with wings on each side. Rotten adjusted his uniform while grumbling, "Marines had to take the greens away from us, didn't they?"

"Marines?" Calvin asked confused as he closed his locker up. Lane paused before telling him, "Consortium is reforming the Corps so the Navy sticks to flying while they do the ground pounding."

"Anything else I miss?" He wondered. Lane sighed, "Just recovering from the never-ending train wreck that is our lives."

Valery snapped at them all, "Stop being a pack of kill joys. We survived a zombie horde; we can survive anything else this damned universe can throw at us!"

"That was corny," Lane said cracking a smile. Valery nudged her, "It worked, didn't it?"

"You took an upper, didn't you?" Calvin asked as Valery laughed, "You should know."

Calvin paused as Rotten giggled, "You dirty bastard."

"Don't judge me! Who am I kidding?" Calvin

resigned himself to his further shame.

"Degeneracy aside, might as well get this briefing over with. Shall we?" Lane asked them, wanting to change subjects as they filed out of the berthing. Rotten grabbed Calvin's shoulder asking, "So, how was it you perverted bastard?"

"It was like masturbation. Felt good, but a total disgrace afterwards," he told him honestly. Rotten laughed, "Valery or Holly?"

"Yes," he sighed as Rotten tried not to laugh out loud. "Hope it was worth it."

"Was at the time," Calvin told him, knowing about his new son. He focused on the present as they passed through the repaired passageways. The crew was doing touch up work, painting over the patch jobs that had just been completed. Everything looked almost as good as new. The lights working tripped everyone out as they'd gotten used to them malfunctioning. Everything also felt much bigger than before as they had room to move around instead of being crammed in. When they walked into the wardroom, they were surprised to see four giants over eight and a half feet tall and covered head to toe in armor that looked more advanced, better armed, and heavier than anything they had. Two were male and the other two were females. On their heads they had a Mongol symbol. There were multiple weapons attached to them, boosters on their joints, compact jetpack on their backs, and the helmet looked like a face contorted into a smile. Their chest had the Mongolian words for "Be offensive" carved in as well. They stepped aside as Holly was finishing up a conversation with Sophia. Sophia still looked pale as ever and had her white hair put up in a bun. She had on a set of blue coveralls that seemed overly baggy on her small body. They all knew she was an alien, but she still looked almost human. Holly looked up at them and smiled, "Welcome Chiefs. While you're all here, take a good look at real operators. They are more hardcore than any of you all could ever hope to be. Now congratulations on your promotions! You all are the only few that survived the transition to this timeline, avoided being a zombie's next meal and didn't get fried by a supernova."

"Oh, and thanks for the hospitality. Ice Cream was wonderful," Sophia told them with an unsettling sincerity. They looked at each other dreading the fact that they owed their lives to these two morally reprehensible people. Still, all were resigned to the fact that there wasn't much they could do about it. The presence of the four giants was a clear message to stay in line. Calvin asked, "Wait, just the four of us? What about...?"

"Your clones don't count," Holly told him with a wink. His eyes went wide as Rotten once more tried not to laugh. Valery spoke up, "Ma'am, I'd like to stay with Calvin's fire team. I do understand we're short manned, but we'd be more..."

"Only if you allow those clones in your belly to be extracted and accelerated." She pointed at her stomach. Valery paused, "Huh...?"

"Done it before. Pop them out early, force them to grow up quick, and make them resentful with the truth. Painless save the emotional grief. Only way I'm accommodating you."

"I'm..." Valery was shocked as the giants started laughing loud enough to be heard outside their suits. "Our educational system failed you all. Yet again Calvin never seems to have protection when it matters the most. So do we have an agreement or is more humiliation required?"
"Agreed, ma'am," she told her, accepting the situation. Calvin blushed hard as he started to feel embarrassment again. "Lighten up and take a seat," Holly told them.

They all took their seats as Holly activated a holographic projection, "Alright, the reason we're back in the Sol system is to take it for ourselves. There's a long set of hoops we must go through to make that happen. First, we need to locate some old friends of ours."

She pulled up images of six people that made Calvin's eyes go wide, "You've got to be fucking kidding me?"

"Save the freaking out for later," Valery replied trying to calm him down while being stern. Lane asked them, "Who are these people again?"

"What did they do to get under you all's skin? Piss in your cereal?" Rotten joked with them as Calvin replied, "Alec Dumont, Jane, Kathryn, Yeager, Mira and Connor McCormick. Those bastards tricked me, used me, and then sent me off to die. Vera… never met her. Shouldn't we be looking for that Doctor that doesn't like to give his name out? Pretentious prick. Wait a second. Where's Vera?"

"One thing at a time. First, from what we're able to gather, Doc was last seen on the Pandora. Everyone else was on Earth. When shit hit the fan in this system, the Pandora vanished while in orbit of Earth. At least one of these people would have a homing device for the Pandora to respond to."

"No zombies in this system we need to worry about?" Rotten thought aloud. Holly paused for a second, "No. Zombies would have been less depressing than what happened. Only threats that we are aware of are Valkyrie patrols."

"You mentioned a needle in an empty barn. Guessing you weren't talking about the Pandora?" Calvin asked her. The other three looked over at him wondering what he was talking about. Holly answered, unphased by the question, "You won't be down there just for the Pandora. While it's especially important you do find that ship, it's just the hook for the bait."

Sophia smiled at them, "Don't forget you all owe me. I'm just asking you for a small bit of effort on your part. Follow our lead, and the variables will work out for us."

"Please with sugar on top, cut to the chase and tell us what you want?" Valery asked her, feeling frustrated by

17

the vague answers. Sophia shrugged, "Alright. I have a counterpart in this galaxy in a position I want and I'm going to take it from her. When I'm in that position, I can write off all that you do as Claw activity and allow you to do your own thing in this system. Still owe me one more favor to be named later. Unlike those giant buffoon Claws, I'm not putting my home world at risk."

Holly chimed in before anyone could protest, "Before you all get bent out of shape about throwing the Claw under the bus, they're willing to see us all dead for their own gain. Also, really think they'd let us go after destroying their capital system?"

She looked at each of them seeing their dismay by the revelations being presented to them. "You all wanted to live. This is the price that must be paid. Now to address the elephant in the room, I know you all think of me as a soulless witch. I saw an opportunity to live and took it. You all willingly followed me despite only being half committed. You all are now, so act like you want to win. This is the last time you all must act like bait. The upcoming suicide mission to place Sophia where she wants to be is voluntary. Is that not fair?"

"Sounds like a damn fine deal. Only must do half the work but claim all the glory, while making none of the sacrifices," Sophia condescendingly put it. Calvin realized what she was talking about and nodded, "Fine. Sounds fair and all, ma'am. If you please, tell us what's required then besides a scavenger hunt."

"Does he speak for all of you? I don't want any more interruptions or reservations." Holly asked them. Lane looked over at Sophia, "What's to stop her from…"

"The future favors you all will owe me when this succeeds will prevent you from being squashed like a bug. How many more times do we need to repeat ourselves until you all understand? Are you listening to me?" She sarcastically asked them, vocalizing her annoyance.

Lane scoffed, "New boss is same as the old boss."

"Don't compare me to those dumb lizards. I have a functional brain where theirs is still underdeveloped." She smiled at them almost laughing.

Rotten sighed, "We don't need to worry about the same thing happening again like in the last suicide mission, right?"

"What part of that suicide mission being voluntary don't you all understand? We're calling what occurred a miracle for a reason." Holly pushed the point of how lucky they were to have figuratively gotten a mulligan.

Before Lane could ask, Holly guessed her question, "These operators are a last resort. Not to mention, your gene pools are being tested to see if they're worth being added to their stock. Lastly, the abilities that you all used might have adverse consequences, so use them sparingly. Understand?"

"Is there anyone left saving in this system?" Valery asked. Holly paused for a second looking at the holographic display. For once she wasn't being feisty and looked genuinely troubled as she composed her thoughts, "We only need to save ourselves as usual. We've entertained your questions enough. Just get this right and you all can choose for yourselves what you want to do next. Do I need to repeat myself?"

"No ma'am," Calvin told her in begrudging agreement. Holly grabbed four data pads and handed them out, "Capture a Valkyrie operative, take her to the Pandora, get that ship back in operation, and act as bait. Process the information and share it with your fire teams in four hours. Dismissed."

The four of them stood at attention and filed out of the room. Once the door was closed to the passageway, Rotten sighed, "If only this was voluntary."

"Scared about what we might find on Earth, Rotten?" Lane asked him as he sighed, "More of what we won't find."

"Take everything that was said with a grain of

salt," Valery looked back in suspicion.

Calvin sighed as he dreaded looking at the information he needed to know. Valery patted him on the shoulder, "I'll meet you later. Don't judge yourself too harshly."

He nodded as the four of them broke off. Calvin waited until he was alone to start looking at the data pad. He psyched himself up to take a look. When the images started displaying in front him, Calvin quickly realized what was wrong. "No one is there…"

Chapter 3
Brief Some
2272
Sol System
C.S.W. Jason
Classroom 2

ALVIN grumbled while resentfully accepting his situation, taking his time going to the classroom. The lights were too bright, and he felt sick to his stomach. Trying to get his mind off the intel, he took a quick look at his holographic pad to see who'd be under his command and gasped at the names, "What?"

He saw his son Hail, who was already a man. He had very dark skin, short black curly hair, a sizable jaw, one blue eye with the other golden, and an average sized nose and mouth. Then there was Lane and Rotten's daughter, Barbra Rotten. She had similar facial features to her mother save pale skin and green eyes. Lydia Oleg was blonde with a symmetrical face, lightly tanned skin, and blue eyes. Audie Spencer had wide eyes, blonde curly hair, a wide jaw, mouth, and thin nose. Zen Keaton had brown hair, pale skin, brown and blue eyes. Zen, Audie, and Barbra were all Lance Corporals in the newly reformed Marines, while Hail and Lydia were both crewmen in the Navy. Calvin saw that they were only hours old at best. He rose his hand up to his face and gasped to himself realizing that they had their aging accelerated. Calvin looked at his reflection in the metal in front of him seeing his hair had gone gray, his skin was pale, he had bags under his eyes, and he looked thinner than before. "Oh, fuck me. What have I done?"

"Is that an invitation?" Helena asked him flirtatiously. He gasped seeing her as she laughed, "Relax, I'm just a figment of your deteriorating mind. Guess it's true that they grow up quick."

"Great. Nice to know I'm losing it," he told her in dismay. Calvin looked around for Valery wondering when she was going to show up. Helena smiled, "Aw, miss your friend already? Also, you know it was gross fornicating with yourself, wasn't it?"

"So, I figuratively masturbated in a more literal sense. It's just as bad," he told her honestly. Helena nodded, "You went full pervert. Never go full degenerate. I was just starting to like you."

"You are a figment of my mind. Seeing how I'm talking to myself… again… what am I supposed to tell them? They all probably have phony memories. So, should I tell them that Krampus doesn't exist or let them believe in a judgmental monster?" he asked her out of desperation. She sighed, "Just tell them the truth. Santa is the one that doesn't exist."

"You know I don't want to have another…" Calvin paused thinking about his first son, Yeager. He couldn't say his name knowing the world he was left in. Helena sighed, "The Yeager of this timeline was never your son. The man you're thinking of left you to the wolves. Stop with the weepy bitching and do your job."

Calvin looked at her confused and shocked by her bluntness. "You want comfort? Valery seems to be giving it to you. I'm your damned resolve to get shit done." She patted him on the shoulder. Calvin asked, "Am I still high? Everyone is being straightforward for once and not coy."

"No need for lies when you're out of the pan and into the fire. Your guess is as good as mine. Again, imaginary friend right here," She told him as he grumbled and rubbed his eyes, "Right."

22

When Calvin looked again, she was gone. Out of paranoia, he double checked to make sure no one else was watching him. He nodded and started moving again towards the classroom. He couldn't help but jump every time he heard a noise, partly thinking zombies still wandered the vessel. The passageways were empty with most of the crew and ship riders in their own compartments, probably going over what needed to be done soon. He tugged down on his coveralls, partly missing the comfort from the armor he wore. Valery walked up to him looking like she was hollowed out, both figuratively and literally. Calvin gave her a hug, and she sighed, "Forgot about consequences while being drugged up. Always a price to pay."

Calvin laughed weakly as he patted her on the head, "We're alive, so we did something right. We can't keep postponing this forever."

Valery moved back, straightening out her coveralls and composing herself. "After you, team lead."

He gave a smile as he opened the door. He quickly psyched himself up by telling himself, "I got this."

They went into the classroom where the new team was waiting for them. Jokingly, they all stood up and shouted, "Attention on deck!"

Calvin laughed, "Very funny. I work for a living."

"Saying officers don't?" Hail asked him, smiling. Barbra laughed, "Paperwork isn't going to push itself."

Calvin nodded, "Targets aren't going to get shot either if we just clown around. Take your seats."

They all sat down and looked up at him waiting to hear what he had to say with eager eyes, itching for action. The anticipation was practically written on their faces. Calvin placed the pad on the wooden podium. He took a deep breath and made up his mind on what to tell them. "Before we get started…"

"Focus on the mission," Valery interrupted in frustration, just wanting to get it over with. The others looked at each other in confusion. Calvin rocked his head side to side, "No. Addressing this elephant right now. Your lives literally just began a few hours ago. Your aging was sped up, and your memories are fake. I'm not holding back any information from you all. If you need a moment to process this information, I'll give what I can."

Zen, Hail, and Lydia looked more disappointed than shocked, "Damn it!"

While Barbra and Audie were laughing, "We won the bet!"

"You all are a pack of sick fucks for gambling on existentialism," Valery commented, both impressed and dismayed by their wager. Barbra sighed, "Lighten up. No point in worrying about things we had no control over. Oh, you all have to clean our gear for the next month."

"Deal is a deal," Hail said in dismay. Calvin was slack jawed in surprise, "You all are good sports about this."

"We've all had our perspectives on our lives shattered and we're about to go on a life-or-death mission. Kind of have to be thick skinned," Audie told him.

He nodded, "That was less painful than I thought it would be... no offense."

"None taken," Lydia told him. Calvin composed himself and started showing off the holographic images of the system, "If you all don't already know, we're taking back our system."

Earth was magnified and zoomed in on. "We're one of four fire teams that will be looking for Valkyrie operatives to capture and we'll also locate the Pandora. We're heading to a potential hot spot around New Seattle in North America. Any questions?"

"What's so important about the Pandora? She's probably been out of commission for some time," Hail pointed out. He looked over at the familiar star shaped vessel as it spun around. "Dragon's Teeth. Supposed to help us rebuild."

"I think we'd be better off going to a different system. Earth looks dead," Audie pointed out. The world looked barren and inhospitable. The oceans were almost black, the forest seemed burnt out, and the cities were all dark lifeless husks. Calvin said heavily, "Never give up on the home world."

Barbra asked, "What do we do when we find survivors?"

Calvin looked at her for a few seconds, thinking of what to tell them, "There's no one to be found."

"Fuck," Zen quietly said. Lydia scoffed, "Oh come on. There's got to be someone there besides the aliens, right?"

"This isn't a rescue mission; this is technically a snatch and grab," Calvin told them all bluntly. Zen spoke up in a high-pitched voice, "Chief, back to us only being a few hours old. Why did I get memories of being abused constantly, and who do I need to kill for being so cruel as to do that to me?"

Everyone looked over at her as she stared at Calvin. His mouth was once more hanging open in dismay, knowing there were still things that phased him, "From abuse strength... or your makers were just being jerks by giving you bad memories to motivate you to kill."

"Jerks," she quickly told them.

"Anyone else have anything?" He asked them once more as they calmed down. Audie motioned, "Shouldn't we know the capabilities of the Valkyries we're going up against, Chief?"

"Right," he told him, pulling that information up. He felt frustrated that he didn't have his brief better organized. Images of robots popped up. They looked humanoid with a round dome as a head, dark colored slick metal, and multiple weapons on their body. "Valkyries mostly use battle bots to do their fighting. We'll have to go through them first to capture our target. From the information... we were provided," Calvin paused to not use Sophia's name, "They operate in twelve-man fire teams and within proximity to transports or gunships, depending on the situation. They're more than likely just making sure hazardous items are being disposed of. We'll get the drop on them and fuck up their shit before they even know what hits them. Any other questions?"

"New Seattle is huge. How are we going to find alien droids in a massive city like that?" Lydia asked him. Calvin looked over the information, "Elements that aren't natural to our world will be easier to detect. Think of a dog sniffing out a scent. We're going in light on our feet to cover more ground faster. With that in mind, manage your equipment and ammunition. If we don't have any sign of the Pandora after we capture the asset, we'll head to the nearest extraction point. We have contingencies in case things go wrong. I'd like to not drag the big scary operators in to save us on our first mission together. Before we gear up, anything else?"

"No Titans?" Hail asked with a bit of disappointment in his voice. Calvin laughed, "They aren't for subtlety. Now let's go capture a Xenos."

CHAPTER 4
HOME COMING
2272
SOL SYSTEM
C.S.W. JASON
HANGER BAY

OES it normally take eight hours to wait for a ride?"
Audie griped impatiently. Calvin sighed, "Sometimes
longer. Hurry up and wait still applies to us."

"Got to love military logic," Lydia said while
taking a drink out of a flask. Hail asked her, "Wait, we're
not allowed to drink that right before a mission. Are we?"

She offered him a different flask, shutting him up
as he pocketed it. Calvin sighed, "Don't take too much.
Need you all functional. Remember, we might be down
there for a while. Ration it out."

He leaned back against the bulkhead, using his
helmet as a pillow. Their armored suits seemed to be a
downgrade from the last models in the fact that they're
one-trick ponies. Calvin couldn't help but lament the loss
of his multifunctional suit. He figured it was because of
limited resources or more than likely, it was that the
Operators got the high-end gear to themselves. "Bummer
about the old suits. At least we're armored up again. I was
feeling naked without them."

"You seemed comfortable that way," he told her as
she punched him. Audie smirked, "Oh behave."

"You wish," Valery told him as Barbra asked her,
trying to think of the right phrase, "Why aren't you leading

a fire team like your... sister?"

"I want to be with the few friends I have left. Only thing keeping me together. Okay?" She quickly told her.

Calvin nodded, "I think we should do another check."

"We did it five times already!" Audie complained as Barbra mentioned to him, "You're the one that forgot to grab spare batteries."

"We had enough juice," he told them defensively. Calvin told him firmly, "What part of 'this could take a while' did you not understand? You also forgot your combat knifes and extra ammo."

"Are we even going to need any of that stuff?" He tried once more when Lydia kicked him in the crotch. Thankfully, he had installed his armored plates correctly. "Better to have it and not need it; instead of needing it and not having it."

"Might have all day but stop dragging heels," Calvin reminded them as they started checking each other's equipment. Though all their suits were the lighter models, each of them had specific customizations. Hail, Calvin, and Zen all had on suits with extra boosters attached to make them go fast and be nimble. Audie and Lydia had on stealth cloaks that made them practically invisible. Lydia carried the sniper rifle while Audie would be spotter. Valery and Barbra's suits had a back mounted cannon that could be swung over the shoulder and fired. All of them brought as much ammo as they could carry just in case. Even though each magazine held up to two hundred rounds, shots were determined by how much power was available for each energized projectile round. Valery sighed, "Thought we were trying to be light on our feet and quiet?"

"Nothing wrong with bringing some extra fire power," Calvin replied, "What's up?"

"Been hallucinating. Guessing you have, too?" She asked him, already knowing the answer. He sighed, "She tells me that she's my resolve."

"Feels like we're getting pushed off a cliff," she told him honestly as they made sure their suits were put on properly. Calvin reassured her, "We just need to get this right and we can kick out feet up someplace warm and peaceful for a bit."

"Even you don't believe that's going to happen," Valery told him honestly. Calvin smiled, "One can dream."

They both looked up, seeing a head being attached to a new Titan. They looked nimbler than the last version with more boosters on top of the existing firepower and armor. They all shared the humanoid shape, looking like giants. Green was for the Marines and dark blue for the Navy. Their visors flashed red as they were being ops tested. Hail sighed, "Shame we can't bring those along."

"Again, they aren't meant for low profile," Calvin told him as Zen checked Hail's booster. She didn't say much and always seemed to have a traumatized expression on her face. Zen let out a flinch as Hail started checking her. He paused and calmed her down, "I won't bite."

"Last time I got bit by someone I got rabies," she told him as he looked at her for a second. "Nice to see you got better."

She nodded as he made sure her suit was good to go. Barbra mentioned, "Think the word Titan is overused?"

Everyone shrugged, "Yeah."

"Kind of, but the name stuck with those Mechs. Just be thankful we're not going by Spartan anymore. That name got overused," Calvin told her jokingly. As Audie checked over Lydia, she told him, "Don't get any ideas."

"It's okay for you to try crushing my crotch though?" he told her, insulted by what she said. She smiled, "At least it wasn't a bullet."

"Get a room," Barbra told them as they both flipped her the middle finger. Calvin nodded, "This is going well."

"Not killing each other yet," Valery joked with him.

"Chief, is it true that you helped cause this system to end up in the dumps?" Barbra asked him innocently. Calvin answered with honesty, "Not really, but we did make a deal with the devil to not die. System would be dead with or without us. We just happened to benefit."

Valery sighed, "You may judge harshly, but understand no one makes good choices in a desperate situation."

"Yeah, heard about what you all did. That was straight up fucked up," Audie judgmentally interjected. Calvin scoffed, "You wouldn't be alive if said actions weren't carried out."

"Old man, I don't even think you're on your side when it comes to your actions." Hail pointed out the painfully apparent. Valery interjected, "We chose to live, can't cry about how we managed it."

"Can't undo what's been done. Just try to not be an asshole today and maybe make tomorrow not suck. Okay?" Calvin replied to him defensively.

"Is that what you tell yourself to sleep well at night?" Zen asked him plainly. Calvin laughed, "That's what the drugs and concussions are for."

"That's kind of depressing, old man," Hail told him with sympathy, as he nodded sarcastically replying, "Isn't it wonderful?"

"Fuck, you're supposed to be the uplifting one," Valery sighed.

"Doesn't sound like it. For what it's worth, I understand that you had no control over what was going on and couldn't do anything to change it," Barbra told him with sympathy. Calvin couldn't help but feel regret, "Flexible morals is one way to deal with life."

"That's terrible," Hail told him in disappointment. Valery snapped, "Don't judge us! Who am I kidding?

Judge away."

"Flexible morals. I was told the same thing by others," Zen told him sarcastically. Another voice chirped in their ears, "Fire team Hotel, report to transport one zero six."

"Roger. Let's go," Calvin replied as they all picked up their weapons, making sure not to flag one another as they headed to the flat triangular shaped transport. The new Condors were larger and sleeker than the older models, able to carry two Titans or two platoons of personnel. The hull was smooth and painted black to blend in with space. It could also be configured in multiple ways for various missions. It was rigged up to get them to their insertion with few bells and whistles. The doors on the side of the cargo compartment slid open allowing them to enter. They piled in with plenty of room to move around in the compartment, as it was just the seven of them. When the last person entered the craft, the doors closed, and the transport started lifting back up. Calvin joked with them, "Buckle up. Landing is going to be rough."

"You are a pessimist. I'll bet 20 Digits that we'll have a smooth landing," Audie told him. Calvin laughed, "We're getting paid with drugs."

"Sell your stash on the black market to get some currency," Barbra jokingly suggested. Zen chimed in, "There wouldn't be much of a market seeing how it's legal and you're just kidding…"

"Don't worry. You'll learn," Hail told her patting her on the helmet. The lights flashed red indicating they were about to launch. Everyone got their face masks on and made sure their suits were airtight. Audie asked, "Wait, if we're augmented, then why do we need airtight…"

"Chemicals can still kill us if we're not protected," Lydia told him quickly to shut him up. He nodded, "Oh, point taken."

"I know you're only a few days old at best, but

always expect the unexpected. Pardon me for beating a dead horse, but I can't emphasize this enough. Be on your toes and have your head on a swivel. Frankenstein would have made sure that he wouldn't be easy to find or get to. Seeing how the Valkyries couldn't find him, we're going to have a hard time ourselves."

"Think the Doc saved himself?" Valery wondered aloud. Lydia asked, "Which Doc?"

"Old associate of mine," Calvin answered her question.

"Wait, wasn't it mentioned that we need the former Spartans to find said Doctor and Frankenstein?" Barbra asked him. Calvin grumbled, "That bastard never gave me his name. I'm going with that one. He's not worthy of being called Daedalus."

"Who?" everyone else asked him as Calvin explained, "Father of Icarus."

"Oh." They all realized what he was talking about. Valery laughed, "You know the saying of don't fly too close to the sun, right?"

"Who doesn't?" he replied to her as she mentioned, "There's a second half. Don't fly too close to the ocean."

Calvin paused, "Huh… I'll keep that in mind."

"Stand by for launch," said a voice over the intercom. Letting out another sigh, he nodded, "Let's be offensive!"

CHAPTER 5
BITTER LANDING
2273
EARTH
CONDOR TRANSPORT
CARGO HOLD

W E'RE in for a smooth landing for once!" The pilot shouted with joy as the lights flashed in the compartment indicating for them to stand up. Calvin sighed, "I'll be damned."

"You owe me 20, Chief!" Audie told him jokingly. Calvin nodded, accepting his loss, "Not crashing is a win."

Valery sighed, "Is it strange that I was hoping for it to be rough... wait..."

"Poor choice of words," Lydia told her as she grumbled, "Damn. Walked right into that one."

The pilot chimed in again, "Bad news. Going to take us some more time to land. Sit back down."

"Figures," Calvin scoffed.

Audie shouted, "This is bullshit!"

"Get used to it. We can still crash," Calvin told him, smirking under his face mask. Audie attempted to give him the middle finger but stopped after being pushed into his seat by Hail. He lifted his hands up, "Alright!"

Barbra asked, as they got comfortable waiting again, "That Doctor couldn't take the time to create some kind of IFF?"

"You don't know that Doc," Calvin told her as Valery laughed, "None of us really did."

Barbra nodded, "Okay, how about we get to know each other more. What kind of ice cream do you like, Chief Marley?"

"Rocky road," he answered instantly. She laughed, "That's a popular one, isn't it?"

"You're talking about desserts right now?" Hail asked her, realizing she was just trying to get her mind off the wait. "Mine is lemon lime sherbet."

"That does sound good, especially with extra cream." Everyone took a moment to look over at Zen, "Cookies and cream jerks."

"I'm more of a Neapolitan person myself. Three in one," Audie shouted wanting to distract from the last comment. Barbra smiled, "S'mores."

"They had that flavor in your phony memories?" Calvin asked her as she nodded at him. Lydia sighed, "Here me out, gelato is better than ice cream."

"Well, aren't you just alternative?" Calvin scoffed at her remark as Valery chimed in, "Cookies and cream, too."

"Also, an excellent choice," he told her as the lights flashed again and the pilot told them, "It's cold outside. Make sure you're bundled up. And don't eat the yellow snow."

"I had to..." Zen murmured as the others looked back at her. "Never mind."

"Our makers are jerks." Audie looked at Calvin and Valery, "Don't look at us."

"Dust off!" The pilot shouted as the doors opened. The seven of them quickly ran out into the bright white light and into the open. They landed in the thick snow, sinking up to their knees in the powder. The pilot told them before vanishing in the sky, "Happy hunting!"

"Steady flying," Calvin replied, looking up at the clear dark blue sky. He couldn't help but smile, "Good to be home."

"Don't speak too soon," Valery told him. They looked back down, seeing a vast sheet of snow on top of a large structure. The team was on the very top of it over the massive city. It resembled a metal rainforest with the way the levels stacked up on one another. There were massive pillars that held each section up. They could see the bay as the waves moved around. There were several abandoned ships, boats, and planes along the shoreline. They looked rusted, beaten, and broken down. The whole city did. It looked neglected. Only sound to be heard was the roaring wind as it blew through the empty city. Hail pointed out, "It's quiet."

"Too damned quiet... this city should have millions of people in it... where are they?" Barbra asked trying to keep her composure. Even though they were in some of the best war gear available, they felt like ants on a giant frozen carcass. Calvin motioned for the others to follow, "Come on. We're going down the scenic route. Keep in a single file line. Last man erases our tracks."

They quickly formed up, with Audie doing what he could to cover their path to look like they were never there. All of them headed to one of the few structures visible to them. It stood out like a sore thumb as it was a glass cylinder held together by silver-colored ceramics. As they got closer, they saw it was a museum built around a large elevator showing the history of humanity. The top level would be the latest pinnacle of man's success. They each ventured inside, seeing the history of humankind as shown by artifacts and photographs. The most recent set of pictures showed the construction on the top layer and a model of what it was to look like. It looked lively, open, and festive. Lydia sighed, "What could have been."

"Did we really have to enter through the top?" Audie asked, feeling the emptiness of the place. Calvin sighed, "Think low profile. Okay?"

He nodded while they progressed backwards in humanity's history. They went from the colonies in the system to the digital age, the first space flight to the first flight in general. Combustion cars to the steam engine. Muskets to pikes. Sail boats to row boats. With the light being scattered by the broken glass, there were multiple rainbows visible as they went along. The air was still with snow floating all around. Calvin saw the elevator and moved to open the large silver doors. With little effort, they opened, but he almost fell forward into the empty shaft. Valery pulled him back as he regained his balance, "Want to take the stairs?"

"We have boosters. We can jump down without being seen," Hail told her as he warmed up the boosters. Hail then spoke up, "Dad... Chief... I think you're going to want to see this."

Calvin turned around as Hail was looking at two skeletons wearing warm clothing and a single hole in their heads. "Oh..."

The two bodies were lying next to a photograph of the first rock paintings known to man. There was another drawing underneath it: a group of Spartans standing side by side, seemingly waving goodbye, probably the last drawing of man. Lydia mentioned, "These two were poetic. Also liked to party."

She kicked a stack of bottles and pills. Audie sighed, "Wouldn't you if you could?"

Despite seeing so much death and carnage, something felt wrong. Calvin moved closer to take a better look at them. They were seven feet tall. Their faces were covered up with flight masks connected to long empty oxygen tanks. The two seemed to have fallen while firing their last rounds in vain. There were signs of a fire, empty weapons next to them, and the last of some rations nearby. Calvin let his weapon hang from the strap as he knelt down. He took a closer look at them and saw they had on makeshift suits made from scraps. They both had the old Spartan helmet painted on their right shoulders. The light shined, making two sets of metal ovals visible. "Dog tags?"

Valery moved behind him, "This is already fucked up as it is. Let's just let them lay in peace."

"Someone needs to know who they are," Calvin

told her as he pulled the two sets up. His heads-up display was able to read the names instantly: Vera Marley, Yeager Marley.

"What?" Calvin asked in disbelief at the names he was clearly seeing. Like ripping a band aid off, he reached down and pulled their masks off. The cold had preserved them, making their faces recognizable in an instant. Calvin dropped backwards on his butt in shock. Valery also recognized them. "No fucking way."

"Rest in peace brother and sister..." Hail said, removing his helmet out of respect, "Wish we'd met under better circumstances."

Calvin felt a surge of emotions going through him. He looked up and shouted in a cracked voice of realization, "You knew, you sadistic bitch. You knew they were here!"

The rest of the team looked at each other both puzzled and concerned. Barbra spoke up, "Chief, I think you have a toxic relationship with the Admiral."

"Fuck off!" Calvin snapped at her while punching a dent into the ceramic floor. Valery tried to calm him down, "Cal. Don't let Holly get under your skin. She's messing with you. Also, you don't owe these two anything. One backstabbed you, and the other didn't know you at all. Hell, this isn't our timeline."

"That's a fucked thing to say, even for you!" Calvin pushed her back as he bolted up. Valery stumbled back, "Okay! Sorry I sounded cold... bad pun..."

"Pointing it out doesn't make it any better!" Calvin shouted, looking down, gritting his teeth and clenching his fists. "I know this isn't my time. I know I was dead to them. Alternative timeline or not, they deserved better than this shit!"

"We'll remember them. We'll avenge them. A tantrum isn't going to fix that," Hail tried to reason with him.

"Cal, this Earth would have gotten fucked over with or without us here. Not our fault this happened. I understand Holly is messing with you, yet I got to ask. Are you going to be able to function?" Valery asked, trying to be understanding. Audie suggested, "We can clone them. No big deal."

"People shouldn't be replaced so easily!" Calvin shouted at him, angered by the idea. Lydia was even more crass, "You just made multiple copies of yourself. Who are you to talk about not making copies?"

Calvin started walking up to her when Hail got in the way, "Chief, get a grip. Lydia, really?"

Zen sighed, "Show the dead some respect."

She grabbed a nearby large flag and covered the bodies while weighing it down with what was available. Once she was done, she told them, "We still have a job to do."

"I know they wouldn't shed a tear for me. I know they thought I was dead. I know they aren't mine..." Calvin said again as Valery sighed, "We can't do a therapy session in the middle of a mission."

"Why does life keep fucking me over? I was just following damned orders!" Calvin shouted before getting slapped across the face by Hail, "Tears don't fix shit. Violence does, despite what mother says. Don't be sad, be furious. Wait, my mother would never say that. Well, you got the idea, right?"

"Hail, I don't know if getting him more furious is a good idea." Valery told him as Zen held up a camera she found next to the bodies. Calvin went over to grab it when she handed it off to Hail, "Mission first, Chief. Be angry, but not infuriated... okay?"

"Fine. Let's find these cunts," Calvin said with his sorrow now turning to rage. The team got the doors open wider for the jump. Two by two they made the blind leap down. Calvin took one last look back at the two bodies. All the resentment he had about getting betrayed vanished. He wished deep down that he could have reconciled with them. Valery told him, "Not considering the cloning?"

"I think they had a better fate than we got," he told her, knowing they only died once when he'd die a thousand more times. Valery told him, "Let's make this world something worth living in again."

"Corny much?" He asked her as she sighed, "Someone's got to support your unlucky ass. Let's not leave anyone else waiting."

Calvin saw they were the only two that hadn't jumped yet. He nodded, and they both leapt into the darkness together.

CHAPTER 6
METAL JUNGLE
2273
EARTH
NEW SEATTLE

E'RE on a wild goose chase, aren't we?" Audie asked rhetorically. Lydia grumbled, "Rub salt in the wound, why don't you?"

"If this was a wild goose chase, I wouldn't have found my children dead on this barren rock right after we landed," Calvin told them bitterly. Valery went up to him, "Again, can't let Holly get under your skin."

"Too late. Got to admit she's incredibly lucky with her choices so far..." Calvin said, gritting his teeth. His grief, frustrations, and helplessness were slowly turning to fury burning inside of him. He kept a high pace, wanting to find those responsible for what happened. They safely managed to land on the next level down, right on top of the broken lift. After they exited the shaft, they found a vast maze of abandoned skyscrapers. The light simmered off the glass that remained, illuminating the desolate city. Sidewalks were cluttered with abandoned vehicles, snow, debris, the occasional downed aircraft, and leftover war equipment. Next to the shaft was an abandoned Titan that looked picked apart. It was a microcosm of the decay the city was going through. Most of the metal skin of the main body was ripped off, the internal components were ransacked, and its reactor was ripped out. Audie mentioned, "Chief, if the Valkyries are trying to remove hazardous items, maybe we should go where said hazards are."

"Place looks well picked over. Sure, there's anything left?" Lydia wondered as they ventured past abandoned hover cars and the older variants nearby. It was a blend of modern and obsolete technology lying next to one another. Still, it was unnerving not finding anyone else. Closest things to signs of life were abandoned Spartan equipment. Armored suits were posed like mannequins in random spots. Barbra started altering the setting on her scanner, "I think I got radiation north of here. Want to see what it leads to, Chief?"

"Sure. Good idea as any," he told her almost dismissively as they made a turn. Lydia came to a stop, gasping as she almost fell forward to the next level. After losing her balance, she used her boosters to hop to the other side of the hole. Looking down, they saw it was caused by an old Crain transport that was broken in half on the next level. The others followed suit flying over. Audie gasped, "This city is unsafe as hell! How did people live here?"

"Probably would have had these holes patched up by now. I mean government work is that slow," Lydia joked as Hail laughed, "You'd be surprised."

"How did this city end up like this again?" Barbra wondered as the wind blew through the empty buildings. Only other sound was falling debris that came raining down from broken parts of the structure. Calvin told her, "Valkyrie weapon. Must have killed all advanced technology. They're going to pay."

Hail moved up to him as they walked along, "Old man... Chief. No disrespect, but will you be able to keep your cool?"

Calvin couldn't hide his anger, "I won't kill the little fucker we're supposed to catch. I'm just going to introduce it to pain."

"Mission first," Zen bluntly told him in her almost childish voice. Valery sighed trying to support her friend, "Breaking some bones doesn't go against mission

41

parameters."

"Not inspiring any faith in your emotional states Chiefs. Forgive me, but halt," Barbra told them. Valery and Calvin both looked at her with shock and were about to boil over with anger as Hail lifted his arms up, "Chief, my memories with you might be fake, but you always told me cooler heads prevail..." He paused for a second thinking about his words, "Calmer heads prevail. I'm so sorry."

"I thought I had poor choice of words," Calvin grumbled, getting annoyed with the puns.

"Hail, it just occurred to me that your mother is a complete psycho," Barbra pointed out, getting off subject. Hail laughed, "Just occurred to you?"

"Court martial me. We are literally only a few days old," she mentioned as he nodded, "Fair point."

Calvin spoke, up, "You all can deal with detaining them, and I'll take care of the damned robots. Challenge my authority again, and we're squaring up. Let's keep going."

They others nodded in agreement, satisfied with the answer as they all moved on. The seven of them moved forward in a file formation with Lydia in the front. She scanned the buildings in front of them. Seeing how everything was abandoned, she gradually became more passive with said scans. Zen made sure that they didn't leave any tracks in the show as they moved along. There was the loud boom of falling debris as the city was slowly being weathered away by nature. The place didn't have a single organic aspect to it as everything was metal, glass, cement, or plastic. Lydia spoke up, "I'm picking up alien elements."

All of them had their weapons at the alert position. Calvin had an itchy trigger finger, wanting nothing more than to let rounds fly. The fact that everything was so quiet and they hadn't found anything yet only added to their urge to fight. While pushing ahead, Audie started to speak nervously, "So you mentioned one specific Doctor who's so brilliant, but he couldn't activate this Dragon's Teeth device thing to prevent all this?"

"Couldn't get something activated? Sounds like you on a Saturday night," Lydia joked with a couple others giving a small chuckle. He turned around and used the camera on his rifle to keep looking behind them as he snapped back, "You don't know me!"

"You don't even know you." Barbra pointed out the harsh truth of his existence. He replied in an angry stutter, "Well..."

Hail sighed wanting him to just stop, "Save your existential breakdown for when we're not in danger. How did I end up the adult of the group?"

Lydia wondered, "So is Chief still mad at this Doctor or glad he inadvertently saved you two?"

"Rub it in their faces that they dodged a bullet while people they cared about didn't. Nice," Audie sarcastically told her as Lydia sighed, "My bad."

"Apology is only going to get you so far," Valery told him, unable to hide her annoyance.

"This timeline got picked for a reason. This Frankenstein mustn't have covered his bases well enough. We'll find out soon enough," Calvin told them plainly while focusing on their surroundings. Valery huffed, "Pandora will be nearby, won't it?"

"Holly wouldn't want it any other way," Calvin told her once more fighting the urge to rush ahead guns blazing as his thoughts strayed back to the landing. Barbra wondered aloud, "Franken-who?"

"Now I'm the one with references no one gets. He was a fictional mad scientist, a fitting nickname for the bastard we're looking for. Did you all at least understand the analogy?" Calvin asked them, trying hard to hide his frustration. Zen mumbled, "I hate it when people play doctor on me."

They all paused quickly before shrugging off what

she said. Hail lifted his non-firing finger and asked, "We're not going to…"

"We're all disturbed. Just roll with it," Barbra told him, scanning her field of view. The signal was getting stronger as they went along. Valery nudged Calvin, "I think your son has the hots for basket case, Cal."

"Right. He has better taste than I do," he told her dismissively. Another good gust of wind came along and knocked down more clumps of snow onto the buildings below. They came up to a drop and had to make another jump down. The further they went down, the older the buildings became in their architecture. There was also abandoned military equipment all over the place and signs that battles took place. The structures had bullet holes and craters from explosions, and burn marks littered the place. The ceiling reflected the light from the outside, still illuminating the empty part of the structure. Audie pointed out, "The buildings aren't as tall as the skyscrapers from above. We could save time by leapfrogging the roof tops."

"Don't want to risk detection. Stick to the streets and alleys," Calvin told him even though he thought it would be a promising idea. Lydia raised her hand, "Company is coming."

One more gust of wind blew through the city loudly. The snow soon came falling around them. As it did, they saw a figure only visible by the white powder covering it. Lydia quickly pulled her rifle up and fired. There was a bright flash as something was struck. It was humanoid in shape, but not organic as sparks flew out from the exit wound. The android with its silver metallic skin became visible as its stealth drive shut down. The machine spun on the concrete with a large hole in its chest. It was surprisingly thin. The legs looked like two long claws attached to the hips, and the arms looked like metallic toothpicks held together by rubber bands. The head was a round dome with what looked like a diamond at the center and four glowing eyes on each side of the diamond. Before

Lydia could double tap, the machine let out a loud high-pitched screech. Its head split in half from the round flying through it. Calvin shouted, "Get to cover!"

Hail nodded, "So the Valkyrie have invisible reconnaissance drones?"

"Way to point out the painfully obvious. Some of us need it though," Lydia looked over at Audie. He gave her the middle finger. They all scanned the nearby buildings and the snow falling around them, trying to see if there were more of those machines. Valery took a large broken piece of glass and smashed it on top of the droid, "Make it look like an accident for a few seconds."

"Aliens got to be nearby. Let's find them," Calvin told them, eager for another fight. The team started to sprint down the street, not caring if they made a sound at this point. They were counting on company to come their way. He motioned for Lydia and Audie to move ahead to make sure they weren't running into an ambush. The snow kept on falling around them, carried by the wind. Zen did her best to kept erasing the tracks behind them. The falling ice soon exposed more of the drones popping up around them. "Weapons free!" she shouted.

They all opened fire at the drones when spotted. Valery sighed, "So much for surprise."

Half the drones they fired at managed to dodge the rounds as they flew at them. Hail sighed, "I feel like we're the ones that got baited!"

"There's an idea. Lydia and Audie, go dark," Calvin told him as they quickly blended in with their surroundings. The rest of the fire team kept taking potshots at the machines when they popped up. Using the distraction as the drones harassed the rest of the fire team, Lydia and Audie started marking off the drones, making them visible targets. The team brazenly moved into the streets, firing on the drones around them like they were in a shooting gallery. Calvin wasn't getting the satisfaction he wanted by shooting mindless machines. The oil wasn't the same as blood. Those that escaped the volley started retreated from them, vanishing into the empty buildings. The group kept up their fire, hoping to hit something. Calvin snapped at them, "Cease fire!"

The weapons went quiet with only the sound of snow and wind. Audie and Lydia moved back towards them. Barbra huffed, "Guess they know we're here now, don't they?"

"No shit," Audie scoffed.

Calvin looked up at the shimmering ceiling as the snow hit his face mask, "All part of the plan, isn't it?"

"Plan, what plan? We're just getting left out as bait!" Lydia snapped, with Hail telling her, "When there's bait, there's a trap."

"Now when you say trap…" Audie got cut off went Calvin backhanded him across the face, "Oh shut the hell up! First things last, let's find these fucking aliens already."

Barbra shouted, "Duck!"

They all hit the cement as the snow exposed several more machines. Their fire pinned them down in the streets, as they used their boosters to get to cover in the alleyways. The machines had the high ground and were now pushing the fire team back. As they struggled to not get boxed in, they saw what was firing: a short Valkyrie in a white armored suit. Calvin went berserk, seeing only red. He abandoned his team's position and rocketed up the buildings towards the aliens, ignoring the battle droids around him. The rest of the team didn't have a choice but to follow him and try to provide cover fire. The Alien was in shock over the enraged giant charging at her. He roared loud enough to be heard through his face mask. The alien tried lifting her side arm as Calvin let go of his rifle and pulled out two long knives. Before the Valkyrie could react, her firing arm was sliced in half from the shoulder to the hand. The creature let out a high-pitched scream of pain as her blood froze in the frigid air. Calvin then sliced her other arm in half the same way. He then headbutted her. The alien fell backwards, slamming onto the roof of the building. The hot knives went into her kneecaps with a loud snap. While the alien let out a screech of pain, Calvin shouted, "You are going to fucking die!"

He started stabbing the alien repeatedly in places where it would hurt. Hail and Zen tried to stop him, but it was too late. The alien stopped moving as her torso was crushed. Blood burst from her broken helmet as she gagged to death. He could hear a communication in her helmet in a different language. Calvin ripped off the helmet, "Listen here, fucker! I'm going to rip your fucking limbs off and that of all your fucking kind you piece of shit!"

Valery punched him in the head, "Stop, you crazy fucker! We're getting surrounded!"

The number of droids kept increasing, and the fire team couldn't kill them fast enough. They were getting pushed back by the heavy fire. Calvin saw another Valkyrie operative coming into view to investigate what she'd heard. Calvin quickly put away his knives and shot a couple machines with one hand while lifting the dead body up with another, showing it off. The alien froze in shock at the sight. He let the body fall onto the pavement and made a cutting gesture to the alien before shouting, "Pop smoke!"

All seven of them activated smoke grenades to create a cloud to vanish in. It worked, as the Machines missed their shots. They blindly fired into the fog while they crashed downwards through the street's weak points. They crashed down twice more into a tunnel system and went into a full sprint. Lydia and Audie ditched mines to buy them time. Valery shouted, "Good job, nut case!"

Calvin smiled under his helmet as they ran, "Worth it."

CHAPTER 7
SUBURBIA LINKUP
2273
EARTH
NEW SEATTLE

THE fire team exited the tunnel and dropped down another level. They were getting closer to the surface. They saw signs of survivors that turned against each other, using nothing but primitive equipment to fight one another. The snow made it look like the level was covered in a white blanket. The asphalt roads were now filled with wide cracks from weathering. Most, if not all, of the lamp posts were broken in some way, either from fighting or from neglect. The buildings looked ransacked with the windows all broken, clothing strung out all over the place, and furniture thrown around the area. The hover cars were abandoned in random places on the streets, rusting where they crashed. All were empty. It kept unnerving them that they weren't finding any bodies or signs of the people that were once in the city. Now with the wind and snow came the sounds of alarms from the machines patrolling the city. They knew they weren't alone anymore. The team stuck to the alleyways to avoid detection as they checked their gear after the last fire fight. Hail plainly pointed out, "Chief, you didn't keep your shit together."

"I apologize for making it too quick," Calvin told him, unable to hide his glee at killing the alien, "Don't worry, we'll find another one."

Valery punched him in the face mask, "Stop being an asshole!"

"Yeah, cut the psycho shit out! Fuck me! Hail, why did your bitch of a mother knowingly place them where they'd find Yeager and Vera?" Barbra asked in dismay to Hail, "A test probably. You aren't doing so hot, old man."

"We're not dead. They will be," Calvin said smiling at him, itching to fight once more. He felt a surge of energy as the stimulants and adrenaline made him hyper. A thick fog started to roll into the city, slightly obstructing their vision. "Lydia, check for more tin cans."

"We can't have you going Ahab on us!" Barbra snapped at him. Valery laughed, "You knew that reference?"

"Missing the damned point!" She snapped back.

Each of them kept checking their heads up displays to make sure that none of the patrols were nearby. Audie scoffed, "How the hell did you all survive a zombie apocalypse?"

"By not being fucking weak!" Calvin snapped at him before asking, "Any sign of more Xenos for us to kill?"

"Capture. I'll groin kick you if you snap again," Valery told him as he laughed, "We'll see."

Valery grabbed his shoulder, "Do I have to relieve you?"

Calvin was about to attack her when Hail stopped him, "Save it for the Xenos… we only need one alive. We can't hurt them if they're dead."

"Fair point," he told him, calming himself down. Barbra snapped, "Sorry to be an asshole, but in the opinion of this newborn, Chief Calvin Marley needs to be relieved. Set up or not, he's going to get us killed."

"Our objectives are flexible," Calvin told her through gritted teeth. Zen told him, "Being a blue falcon is lame. Don't fuck us over."

Those words managed to get through to him as he looked at the rest of the fire team. "Okay! Fine. We'll take the next one in alive. Someone else grab them and keep them away from me. Roger?"

"Copy," they replied. Calvin nodded, keeping himself composed as Audie wondered, "Weren't the Spartans of recent times technologically advanced? How did they get caught off guard?"

"Hubris, bad luck, take your pick," Lydia guessed.

"We don't fucking know the specifics. Now I know how Holly felt having to explain everything," Valery replied. Barbra wondered, "Again, didn't this area have millions of people living here? Shouldn't there be bodies at least?"

Valery coldly told her, "Nothing we can do for them. Need to keep going."

"Keep the wild goose chase going?" Lydia asked him bitterly. Barbra told her jokingly, "Don't act like you had anything better going on."

"I was going to get intoxicated thank you very much," Lydia told her as Zen mumbled, "You were just going to cry in a corner."

"What?" They both looked over at her as she kept walking like nothing was said. Audie asked, "Who thought it would be a good idea to give combat training to a mentally abused shut in?"

"Same people who thought it would be a good idea to give those abilities to a cry baby," Zen told him with everyone else cracking up. Audie grumbled, "Okay, that was a good one."

"That's what your mother said last night." Zen told him as he looked back at her and paused, "Wait, what?"

"Kind of sad how she knows your mother better than you do," Lydia nudged him. Hail sighed, "You need to work on your jokes."

"Yeah… jokes." He looked over at her as she cracked up laughing. He smiled under his face mask. Barbra commented, "Audie, I think the crew of the Jason knows your mother better than you do."

"Like your parents aren't a pack of sluts either,"

Audie snapped back at them, getting tired of being the butt of the joke.

"Forgive me, but isn't this an inconvenient time for jokes?" Hail asked looking around at the abandoned buildings and destroyed cars around them. The snow was still coming down, creating an avalanche from the upper levels. Calvin told him, "Laughter is a good distraction from pain. You'll learn."

"Incoming," Barbra gasped as they all scrambled to find someplace to hide. It wasn't easy to find a spot with their signs and bulk. They all managed to find a spot just as multiple diamond shaped vehicles came flying overhead. If it weren't for the snow, they'd be practically invisible to the naked eye. Three of the craft stopped nearby them with multiple drones coming down to the cement sidewalks. Their impact sent vibrations through the asphalt. These models were larger and better armed than the ones that came before. The humanoid machines had silver armored plates, a head with cameras to see 360 degrees, and their hands held a large cannon. They started fanning out with a Valkyrie behind them. She seemed to be focused on tracking a signal. Her suit was silver, and her helmet looked like the machine's head with a diamond in the center and four eyes on either side. The transports hovered up above, giving them air cover. The aircraft didn't make a single sound as they seemed to drifted in the air. Calvin looked around the best he could as the machines started flipping over cars. He quietly asked, "Barbra, think that tracking thing could be reversed to find us?"

"Maybe..." she told him when the vehicle she was hiding under got flipped over, exposing her. She quickly shot the machine multiple times before it could react. It split in two with sparks flying from each half. The other machines immediately opened fire on her as she rolled away into a building for concealment. It did nothing to stop the rounds from going through the steel and concrete. Barbra threw a flash bang to buy herself time. As she kept moving, the doors on the transports opened with snipers taking aim at her. Calvin and Valery got their attention by taking pot shots at them. While he kept them distracted, Hail saw an opportunity. He shouted, "Zen, follow my lead!"

She nodded at him. They both went flying up into the air, throwing the cars on top of the incoming robots to stall them. Their boosters rocketed them up towards the transports in an instant. Hail and Zen both took on different ships as they split up. They managed to catch the sniper by surprise as he got yanked out and thrown down into the streets. They threw every explosive they had into the cockpit and leaped off. They cleared the blast area just in time as the grenades went off. Both transports blew up from the inside out and headed towards the third one. With a loud bang of the ships crashing into each other, they dropped down into the nearby bay. There was a plume of smoke and a large splash from the crash. Lydia and Audie scrambled to get out of the way, shooting the nearby robots in the legs and leaving them to get crushed by falling debris. A couple of the damaged buildings gave out and collapsed in on themselves. This filled the streets with clouds, giving them concealment. Taking advantage of the disarray, Calvin used his back mounted cannon to cut all the machines down in front of them. They ripped apart from their torso, getting split open from the rounds bursting through them. The others quickly started picking off the damaged machines. Barbra laid down cover fire from the roof of the building she was on top of, using her cannons to blast away at the machines at close range. Soon the whole platoon was decimated, leaving the short alien alone. Zen landed in front of her as she turned around and shouted, "No!"

"I was always told no meant yes," Zen mocked the alien as Hail landed next to her. The others soon swarmed around the Valkyrie. Barbra got in between the alien and Calvin who wanted to kill her, "Not this time!"

The Valkyrie tried to go for her side arm, but Zen grabbed it and threw it over her shoulder. The alien shouted in her language, looking at the tall, armored behemoths as they walked up to her. Zen then pulled the computer off her wrist and dangled it in front of the alien mockingly. Audie pulled her helmet off. She had pale skin, white hair that went down to her shoulders, and light blue eyes. Lydia scoffed, "Why would you all go by the code word Valkyrie? You don't look like a fighter."

She smiled at them, "I think you all have a saying of don't judge a book by its cover."

She quickly punched Audie in the stomach, lifting him off his feet and following it with an upper cut as he came down, knocking him flat on his back. Hail tried to punch her, but she moved out of the way and shoved his head into the asphalt. Calvin tried bolting in, but he got hit with a car thrown at him. She used her leg as a springboard to kick both Lydia and Barbra in the head. Both were on their backs seeing stars. Valery took a couple pot shots at her while trying to close the distance. She managed to duck behind Zen not allowing her to get a clear shot. Zen swung around just missing her as she leapt backwards grabbing her weapon. Barbra shoved Zen out of the way as the alien fired, knocking her down. Her armored suit took the brunt of the blast, but she wasn't getting back up. Zen used her boosters to dodge the rounds coming from the Valkyrie. She kicked a car and sent it flying towards Zen. She ducked down out of the way. When the car passed over her, the alien leaped right on top of her, shoving the muzzle of the pistol right under her chin, "Shit!"

"No one move!" she shouted as the others were getting back up. Calvin lifted his hands up into the air trying to think of something. The alien lifted up the helmet to Zen's face, "You primitives actually survived and relearned how to use your broken pathetic equipment? I don't think so. Where did you all come from?"

Barbra shouted at her, "From your mother's place.

53

We ran a train on her!"

"She was a nice lady," Zen told her with the muzzle still digging into her chin. She huffed, rolling her eyes, "We were born in pods you antiquated beasts."

"Got to hand it to you. You're a good fighter. Why use robots?" Calvin asked her, trying to stall for time. He was still trying to think of something when the alien spun Zen around, using her as a shield. The alien snapped at them, "Because we shouldn't have to get our hands dirty with animals like you! You'd all be better off being extinct! Damned creatures don't seem to know when to stay dead! Speaking your disgusting tongue makes me want to chop mine off. Now you all better start answering my questions or…"

Before she could finish, she was suddenly lifted into the air with both her arms snapping violently. The pistol flew of her hands as she let out a loud shrill scream from the pain. Valery became visible standing behind her laughing under her helmet, "You were saying?"

Zen fell forwards and rubbed her chin, "Thanks."

The alien cursed them in her language of screeches. They were soon replaced with even more screaming as Valery put more pressure on her broken bones. "So, you twats do feel pain? That's wonderful."

Barbra stood up holding her chest where she was shot, "Don't kill this one!"

"I want to…" Valery said causing her more pain as Zen struck the Xenos with a sensitive, grabbed her away from Valery and restrained the alien's limbs. "Not this time."

"Chief, I'm picking up a homing beacon from the Pandora!" Lydia said in shock. Calvin huffed, "Maybe we're not alone after all. Let's go before her friends show up."

"Remember, just need one," Barbra told him as the fire team headed towards the bay.

Chapter 8
Dive
2273
Earth
Old Seattle

THE group started to make their way into the ancient city. It was flooded and the first four stories of each building were submerged. Windows had been replaced with ice covering them. Some were partly collapsed from the erosion, weathering, and neglect. There were floating houses and cars in the bay drifting wherever the tide took them. Boats and ships were stuck on the beaches with holes torn into them letting the waves softly make impact with their broken hulls. There was no life to be found in the bay: no seaweed, albatrosses, or fish. The once green planet seemed to have all the life sucked out of it, with metal scabs the only thing remaining of what was. Cloud covered skies turned red as the sun slowly set in the west. Calvin looked at how high the water level was and knew that the levies built were all broken. The Xenos squirmed in Barbra's arms before letting out a muffled scream as her broken bones had pressure put on them again. "Little fucker is waking up?" Barbra asked sarcastically, "Give me another excuse, shrimp!"

"Pandora is here," Calvin spoke up, still looking out at the bay, "What we're looking for is in plain sight."

"Hardly call underwater plain sight," Audie joked.

"Best place to hid it as any," Valery told him as Hail looked at the frigid water, "I like swimming as much as the next person, but I don't know if our suits can keep us warm."

"Don't be a wuss," Calvin jokingly told him. They walked on top of the metal beams with floats under them to keep them above the water. They had to watch their footing as they climbed up to one of the nearby buildings. Hail almost fell over. Zen caught him and kept him upright. He smiled at her, "You saved my life."

"Really?" she asked with joy in her voice and a smile. Lydia spoke up, "If you two need a room, there's plenty to choose from."

The Valkyrie seemed to gag at the notion. Audie laughed, "Not into fornication? You should try it sometime. It's fun!"

"Use sanitizer as lube," Lydia told him as they both laughed. The Xenos looked genuinely scared with wide eyes. Barbra laughed, "Don't knock it until you try it, tinny."

Again, the small alien tried to break free only to get pressure applied to her broken limbs. Zen then moved over to the Valkyrie, "I think we have some time for interrogation. Your friends don't seem to care about you seeing as how there's no cavalry coming for you yet."

"Question while we walk. If she screams, break her jaw," Barbra told her as they kept moving along. Valery moved back and reached for the rubber gag, "Give me an excuse."

She removed the rubber ball, and the small alien growled at them. Calvin laughed, "Aw, it's trying to be intimidating."

"Fuck you animals!" It snapped at them before Barbra once more put pressure on its limbs, with Valery covering her mouth so the screams would get muffled. She then displayed the footage of Calvin violently stabbing her friend to death. "We're not messing around. Now, why did you choose this system to test out your weapon?"

She moved her hand with the Xenos still gasping, "We needed a test site. We got the bonus of exterminating a potential threat, too. You apes don't deserve space."

"Where are the bodies of those that lived here?" Calvin asked her, trying to keep his temper in check. She huffed, "You mean Biowaste? We're cleaning up this planet of garbage. Not much to clean up as you animals ate each other like the savages you…"

Valery covered her mouth as Barbra put pressure on her wounds again. After ten seconds of muffled screaming, Valery removed her hand as the alien vomited, "You damned primitives!"

"What did you do when you found survivors?" Calvin asked trembling with rage. Hail sighed, "That's enough."

"Target practice. Sport shooting. Aim improve…" once more she was squeezed, and the gag was placed back in her mouth. Zen scoffed, "Lovely species."

The ceilings of the upper city started to dim as the sun got lower in the sky. The water would freeze as they hit the shoreline with the temperature dropping. Risking a shortcut, they walked on a roof top that seemed rickety at best. There were multiple holes in it. The surface was ice covered. Each step felt like the floor would give out from under them, not to mention the crunching of the ice. For once, having heavy power armored suits didn't feel that safe to have on. Zen purposely slammed her metal boot against the boards to show them it was stable enough. The sky was becoming dark, leaving them to turn on their night vision. Calvin got closer to Valery, "I know it's been said if something is too good to be true, it is. Don't you think it's a bit coincidental that Pandora now pops up?"

"Got any better ideas on our next course of action?" she asked him. Calvin sighed, "Point taken."

The Valkyrie in Barbra's arms started to kick and squirm while shouting through the gag. Lydia laughed, "Maybe she should go for a swim!"

The alien kept on kicking and squirming. Valery lost her patience, grabbed the small alien out of Barbra's arms, slammed her against a metal beam and applied pressure to her neck, "Do we need to break more of your body?"

Barbra yanked the alien out from Valery's arms and placed her in between her torso and left arm, "Don't do that again."

Valery smiled as she gave the alien the middle finger, "Know what this means?"

She scowled at them. Hail grumbled, "You all are kind of sadistic."

"Only kind of?" Audie joked.

Hail looked around as they ventured through the abandoned buildings. It looked like a storm went through the rooms knocking everything around. "Think anyone is alive on Pandora?" Hail asked.

"Well find out soon enough. Keep going towards the signal. Actually, may I see the camera?" Calvin asked him, knowing what would likely be on it. Hail backed away from him, "We're not scavenging around for a third Xenos to capture. I'll give this to you later."

"Waited this long, we can wait a bit longer," Valery told him calming his nerves.

Lydia sighed. "Not too much further to Pandora. Oh shit. We need to hide first," she told them as she dropped into a hole in the building. The others quickly followed suit by hopping inside. They got behind whatever debris was available. As they crouched down, they realized how quiet it was. The only sound they could hear was the occasional crashing waves. The alien started laughing before Barbra tightened her grip, causing the alien pain again. "Get any ideas, your legs get broken next."

Outside, a dozen diamond shaped vessels started to descend, popping into view with the sun behind them. Calvin looked at the alien and asked, "Does that little runt have a tracking device in her skin? Thought we checked her over."

Barbra dropped the Valkyrie on the floor and gave

her a scan, "Amateur mistake on my part. We normally don't take prisoners." Barbra pulled out a knife as the little alien tried to crawl away. Quickly, Zen violently pulled her back by her broken right arm. Zen held her still as Barbra cut out a cylindrical chip from her neck. The alien screeched all the while. Calvin then had an idea, "Hand it to me."

"What?" She looked over at him puzzled as he scanned the alien and created a holographic replica of her. Hail realized what he was doing and mentioned, "I know I busted your chops, but we need you in charge of the team."

"You all need to find the Pandora. I'm the most experienced and can lure them away," Calvin told them as he grabbed the tracker and placed it on him. Audie pointed out, "Resurrection isn't a sure thing here. Jason might be too far off, and Pandora might not work properly, if at all."

"I'm old. Life has just started for you all. Now, wait until the fireworks start and go. I'll take my chances that the Pandora's resurrection system still works seeing how she's broadcasting," Calvin told them. Valery sighed, "I'm coming with you."

"No, Team needs you. Only need one decoy," he told her as she signed, "We go out, we go out together, like it or not."

"We'll be fine. Keep them away from Pandora. I'll keep the camera safe," Hail told them, taking charge of the team.

"You two are batshit insane," Lydia told them as a compliment. Barbra sighed, "Sacrificing yourself isn't going to change anything. You two have nothing to atone for."

"We made a deal with the devil, so I think we do," Valery told her as she quickly checked her gear one more time. Calvin added, "You all will live, and if I can do that, I know I did something right. Now go."

Hail nodded and motioned for the others to follow him as they moved closer to the bay. Calvin looked at

Valery, "Just us now."

"Wouldn't have it any other way," she told him as they boosted up to the roof of the building and started bolting back towards land as fast as they could move. It wasn't long before all the Valkyrie forces were on them. Valery laughed, "They took the bait!"

"We are good lures!" Calvin laughed, as dozens of attack drones landed nearby. They took pot shots, thankfully missing with every round. They didn't want to hit the fake Xenos they held hostage. Valery managed to shoot two before they had to run. The pot shots landed around their feet as they tried to trip them up. Using the boosters, they managed to make great leaps, forcing the droids to hold fire as they tried catching up. Calvin laughed to himself thinking, "Come and get me fuckers!"

"You are losing your mind," Helena told him from unexpectedly. He gasped, "Oh, come on!"

"You see her, too?" Valery asked him, almost tripping over herself. The building behind them was blown up by a rocket. While the debris came back down around them Helena scoffed, "Don't yell at me. You're the one who's going mad. Also, you're going to lose your life if you don't pay attention."

She pointed at the dozen drones that came popping up in front of them, "Mind your situational awareness?"

Calvin and Valery dropped down, sliding on their knees, sweeping their rifle muzzle, aiming at center mass, and firing in bursts at each bipedal machine. Six of them were struck in the torso with a surge of machinery bursting from their back. Three more were damaged with arms blown off. The last three rushed towards them while firing. Calvin boosted himself up to the right, out maneuvering them and firing a grenade round, cutting the first one in half. Valery shot the last two in the head. One of the diamond shaped ships opened, firing heavy weapons at them. The rounds sent them flying off the roof and into another building, crashing right through the walls. They recovered, sore from the landing and realizing the rouse was up. With another round impacting below them, the building started to collapse. They managed to rocket over to the next building but found themselves surrounded by a platoon of enemy machines. Calvin and Valery were pinned down inside the structure, as they tried holding off the ever-growing number of machines. "Regretting following me?" Calvin asked.

"Not for a second!" Valery told them, hitting a droid right in the head. She covered right, and he covered the left side. They stayed low and shot back as fast as they could. No matter how many they destroyed, more kept popping up. Their suits started taking hits as the shields quickly weakened from the shots. In the flurry of fire, their armor quickly started wearing out. Valery was hit in her right leg through, Calvin's left arm was shot off and his kneecaps were blown off. He dropped onto his back screaming from the pain, "Shit!"

Valery tried to help him when her shoulder got shot clean through, "Fuck!"

The machines moved in, shooting them in the limbs once more, leaving them laying helpless on the floor. A Valkyrie with her arms behind her back walked up to them with the machines covering her. She knelt next to them, "Where is she, monster?"

Calvin started laughing as she pulled his helmet off, "Where is she, you damned animal?"

"She's getting double teamed!" Valery shouted before a droid picked her up and slammed her next to Calvin. Both were gasping in pain as Calvin nudged her with a grenade on his waist. "Didn't think you'd get that reference. You'll love this one. It's a blast!"

Valery pulled the pin.

CHAPTER 9
REUNION
2273
EARTH
OLD SEATTLE BAY
PANDORA
RESURRECTION BAY

ALVIN woke up bursting out of the pool he was in, screaming and still feeling pain. His eyes had trouble adjusting as he floundered about breathless. The liquid around him felt slimy and tasted like salt and vinegar. When he finally felt a surface, he pulled his naked body onto the deck gasping in a panic, remembering where he just was. He saw the number 6A imprinted on his arm. There was a single cord pulled from his belly, as he felt a shock. Valery laughed, "It worked!"

"Take that, fate!" Calvin laughed; happy he wasn't dead for good. Both were freezing as the ship was frigid. All around them was abandoned gear from the Spartan force along with several dead bodies. Looked like they died when the ship crashed. They climbed out of the pool and cleaned the gunk off themselves. Valery sighed, "Is it just me, or am I the only one still feeling too much pain?"

Through the numbing cold he did feel like he'd just gotten shot and blown up. His head still felt like it was going to burst open. He started donning the old, armored suits. Valery looked at him as he sighed, "They're not going to need it. We do."

"Where's that damned Doctor?" she asked following suit and armoring up.

"Good question," he laughed thinking about his situation and where he was. Ship still felt familiar after all this time being away from her. There was a flash of light before a holographic image of the Doctor popped up in front of them. He bore a striking resemblance to Hail. Doc opened his mouth into a broad smile, "Well, you're not hallucinating this time."

"Hello fucker," Calvin snapped at him feeling resentful. Doc sighed, "I never thought I'd see you again. Also, nice to meet a friend of yours. Still ungrateful after all I gave you, I see."

"You sent me off to die, and now you're the one that's dead, asshole!" Calvin laughed at him feeling vindicated. Doc scoffed, "You're going to calm yourself right now or lose one of your prized possessions."

The temperature plummeted in the room, freezing everything. Calvin sighed, "My apologies."

The room warmed back up. "Spare me the tantrum of getting thrown under the bus. You didn't die… permanently. I need you alive to avenge my death and that of everyone else."

"You weren't able to see this coming and prevent it?" Valery asked him as he sighed, "Bad variables had to go somewhere. This was the timeline that got the short straw. I'd given up hope on anyone showing up. Guessing you two are from another time?"

"Yeah. May we cut to the chase and get this ship back up and running? My team needs a pickup. Now, how did you die?" Calvin asked him as he made sure their armor was on right. Like I said, "Variables weren't in our favor. Damned aliens went through our system like a knife through butter. Every damned system we had malfunctioned at the right time to make it a slaughter. Seeing our ridiculous bad luck, I knew we were doomed. I did a Hail Mary and beached the ship someplace safe.

Sadly, we went too quick. Died in the crash. Oh, we're rising out of the bay right now as we speak. I can multitask. Now I believe my prodigal daughter gave you a message for me?"

"How did you know? Wait, daughter?" Valery asked before figuring it out, "Oh. Only she would be able to find a way out of an impossible situation. Right. Holly is your daughter?"

"That explains a lot," Calvin sighed with realization. Also, why Hail looked just like him. A hallucination of Helena nodded in agreement, encouraging him to say, "Your name is… was Hail Murphy, wasn't it?"

"Surprised you didn't call me Frankenstein or Daedalus. That was the name I had. I'm just a ghost now," he said as his holographic projection flickered.

"Let me guess. Your counterparts are the heroes while you're just the egghead stuck in a lab?" Valery asked him mockingly. The Doctor smirked, "You don't know me very well. I don't feel bad. It's the way I like it. Unlike you two, I don't need the limelight of attention to feel validated. Your need for glory landed you in this mess in the first place. Yet again, you two forgot all about that. Didn't you?"

"Past doesn't matter much anymore. I just want to save my fire team, okay?" Calvin told him wanting to focus on what mattered. Murphy laughed as he jabbed Calvin in the eye, making him move backwards in pain, "What the hell?"

Using Calvin's tear, Doc displayed a holographic message showing Holly, "Hi, Daddy! I can't wait to see you again. I know this will make you proud of me."

"Couldn't be more pleased being able to see her turn the tables and connive her way to the top," he told the holographic projection with a tear in his eye. Calvin asked, "Are there any other twisted family members I need to worry about? Also, first things last, what the hell is the Dragon's Teeth?"

"Dragon's Teeth is a building device that has been constructing ships around the belt. Holly got lucky choosing this timeline. As for my family, it depends on the timeline. However, it's so wonderful to meet new members of said family," Murphy told him, patting his shoulder while the information was being displayed next to him. Then a screen showed the Pandora rising from the icy water back into the sky. As it did, it shot down multiple Valkyrie transports giving the fire team time to board the ship through an airlock. Once they were on board the quad star shaped ship sped up into the sky at high speed. Doc nodded, "Been saving the power and energy for a day like this one."

Hail came on the comms link, "Holy shit, you actually pulled it off! Way to go old man!"

"Grandson!" Doc shouted with joy. "What?" asked Hail in surprise.

"Doc is your grandpa apparently," Calvin told him in dismay. Doc nodded, "Glad to meet new members of the family. Today is a good day to die."

"No, the fuck it isn't!" Valery shouted at him. Doc laughed, "For me. Been so lonely here. This isn't living. It's purgatory. There'll be others to take over. I want an ending to this limbo."

"Why should I feel sorry for you... other than the fact you have environmental controls." Calvin remembered as he was speaking. Surprisingly, Doc didn't show anger but genuine sadness instead, "I watched everything I worked so hard to build die: my hopes, dreams, friends... humanity..." The holographic image flickered. "Being alone with no hope has been fifty years of agony. Not being able to rest, interact with anything and staying dormant this whole time. No way for me to end it either. Knowing that my efforts weren't in vain, I can rest. Just in time for one last fight!" Murphy told them as the ship roared back to life with all the systems activating.

The rest of the fire came charging in with the

Xenos in tow, "Yeah, I think the Valkyries saw us. So… hi gramps." Hail told his grandfather. "So good to see you. We'll make do with what we have. They'll board the ship to save that pathetic weasel."

Alarms started to go off as the intercom announced, "Battle stations! Man, battle stations."

Calvin nodded before realizing, "There's only seven of us… well eight if…"

"I have control of all the ship's systems, including weapons. Just hold them off long enough for Holly to do her thing," Doc told them with a wink. Barbra handed Valery and Calvin rifles to fight with. Before he could say anything, his hallucination of Helena spoke up, "The resurrection on this ship is defective."

"What?" Calvin asked with the others looking at him in confusion before Valery snapped, "What the fuck do you mean defective?"

Doctor laughed, "You all are going mad! Sorry I couldn't warn you about the prototype. Can't extend the mind like the newer models could. One isn't meant to die a thousand times."

"Figures," said Valery, knowing what she'd been exposed to. Calvin sighed, "Valery and I will act as decoys…"

"No. We're fighting, too." Barbra told him. Audie added, "Not sitting on the sidelines this time."

"We're young. We can handle at least one or two deaths," Lydia added. Zen laughed, "Get some."

Calvin smiled, "You're all idiots for following me. Ditch the alien here. Break its legs."

"No need for that," Doc told them as a force field enveloped the small alien. "She's secure."

Hail placed the camera in a safe spot in the room, "Keep this safe, too."

"Can do. Now go."

With a nod, the seven of them started boosting their way to their designated airlock where the Valkyries would try to attack them. As they got closer to the air lock, Helena appeared to him again, "Is the self-sacrifice helping with your guilt?"

"Oh, shut up!" Calvin shouted ignoring everyone else. Zen spoke up, "You're being a lunatic, Chief."

"You're telling me," Calvin said out loud as his hallucination replied, "You're making yourself look crazy."

Shrugging off the feeling along with his pestering imagination, he led the way. It felt like coming home after a long time. It was familiar yet more barren. They got in the airlock and pulled out armored plates that would give them cover. One way shielding would block rounds and allow them to fire back while being protected. The auto turrets came online to assist them. The ship started rocking like an uneven washing machine. Loud bangs could be felt through the hull as the ship was getting pounded by weapons fire. Audie asked, trying to keep himself still, "How long could this Dragon's Teeth thing take to work anyway?"

"None of us know!" Lydia shouted as the rocking suddenly stopped and everything was quiet. Valery sighed, "We totally forgot to ask about that."

"We were preoccupied. One thing at a time," Calvin told her as there was a thud from the door and then spherical sparks started going through the passageway. Calvin sighed, knowing what was to come, "Let the auto turret do its job. We'll pick off the stragglers for now."

"Roger," they replied nervously as they waited for the sparks to stop. They seemed to go on for the longest time as seconds slowed down for them. When the door was blasted open, time picked right back up. From the breach came dozens of grenades flying at the shield. They exploded on impact, weakening it with every blast. The team ducked behind the armored plates. Barbra shouted, "Bastards at least know how to do a breach!"

"We know how to plug!" shouted Hail in defiance

as he realized what he said wasn't inspiring. Audie sighed, "Thought my remarks were dumb."

"Save the bickering for when they're dead!" Calvin shouted at them as several smoke bombs went off. The auto turrets fired into the smoke blindly with their twin barrels. The round caused some of the grenades to detonate prematurely. As the weapon fired, it impacted into another shield, making it flash in the darkness. Their HUDs adjusted quickly keeping them from going blind. Soon a laser round went through the shield and blew up one of the turrets. It went backward into the passageway with sparks flying from the destroyed mechanism. Soon all four of them were destroyed. Calvin calmly ordered, "Pieces of crap. Everyone but Lydia, Valery, and Audie, take turns laying down suppressive fire. You two, shoot them when you see them."

Zen and Hail fired into the smoke cloud blindly for a dozen rounds, and then Calvin and Barbra took over for another dozen. There were a couple flashes as two drones pushed forward holding an energy shield ahead of them. Lydia and Audie both got head shots on them. Valery killed two with one shot.

"Show off."

"Do better."

The shield went down and the other four let loose, shooting down eight more machines before another shield could be put up. Two machines flew towards them with bombs attached to their torsos. They managed to get shot before they got close, but the blast sent all seven of Calvin's team tumbling backwards. Hail and Barbra threw grenades to stall for time as they pulled back. They bounced off the corner and down the passageway as the machines gave chase. Each of them took turns providing cover fire as the rest of the team pulled back. Another set of auto turrets popped up and opened fire on the machines, blasting them into pieces. Zen put up another shield as they made a stand. The robots pointed their weapons around the corner and fired in a concentrated burst at the turrets. Lydia and Audie quickly shot their arms off, but two of the turrets were downed. The rate of fire slowed down, and more weapons popped up firing at the remaining two. Zen used her grenade launcher saying, "This should do the trick."

She fired three bouncing grenades that sent a wave of destroyed machines splattering against the bulkhead. Calvin shouted, "Push them back!"

The team stormed forward. Audie and Lydia both held their triggers down as they went around the corner. The invading drones fell back to where they could for cover. Four of them were hit multiple times and went backwards into the deck. Barbra threw decoys toward the machine. They took the bait and fired at them. The rest of the team charged forward again. Zen and Hail were up front carving their way forward with their rifles on full auto. They didn't bother conserving ammunition as they double tapped each drone. Zen got impatient and started jabbing her rifle muzzle into the heads of the machines in front of her. She struck with such force that the head caved in with sparks flying into the open. Audie reached for one the broken turret guns, swung around a corner, and fired. He used his boosters to stay in place as he held the trigger down. Several of the machines were blasted apart in the salvo. As he laughed with joy, Audie suddenly took a round in the head. Lydia reached over and used the machine gun herself. She charged forward recklessly taking multiple hits as she pushed the machines back. Calvin and Barbra followed close behind. The weapons ran out of ammo, and she switched to her side arm. While firing to her last, she pointed at someone before getting shot in the head. Lydia's body slammed into the deck and backed up, getting shot some more. Zen saw what she was pointing at and rocketed forward. The Valkyrie quickly went for her side arm and tried to shoot her. Zen slapped the weapon making it miss and stabbed the operative in the neck. In a fit of rage, she stabbed the short alien multiple times in the head. She also used the body as a shield as the round came at her. Calvin peeked around and fired at drones that seemed to be fighting harder than before. One of them reached forward and pulled the shield away from Zen. She took multiple rounds to the chest and head. Calvin fired enough rounds to saw that machine in half vertically. His rifle ran dry, and he switched to his side arm keeping up the fire. Barbra shouted, "Pull back!"

Calvin boosted backwards as Hail, Valery, and Barbra laid down fire covering him. Another Valkyrie operative came charging at them. She tried to shoot Calvin as he dodged the round by flying in a circle. The operative shot Calvin in the torso and slammed into Hail. They both started wrestling for a weapon while Barbra kept suppressing the machines as they came at them. Valery landed next to Calvin with a hole in her forehead. Hail shouted, "A little help?"

Calvin shot the operative in the back, giving Hail an opening to shoot her in the head. He threw the body down the passageway with grenades attached. The blast took out another group of machines. The passageway was now filled with broken drone parts drifting in the air. Another operative quickly popped from around the corner and shot both Hail and Barbra in the head, taking them out instantly. Calvin played dead as the operative boosted towards him with the machines taking the lead. Just as she was right on top of him, he shoved his pistol into the neck of the operative and shot her multiple times. The two drones quickly shot him dead.

CHAPTER 10
CHANGING TIDE
2273
ORBIT OF EARTH
C.S.W. PANDORA
RESURRECTION BAY

CALVIN again crawled out of the liquid puddle he was in, "I'm fucking sane! Don't even think about it!"

"Who are you talking to?" Doc asked him. Calvin, realizing he wasn't going to get hosed this time, replied, "Force of habit."

He saw the number 7A on his arm now. He grumbled, "Shit!"

Valery showed her number. It was the same, "Right beside you."

The door in front of him started to open as grenades was chucked inside. Calvin and Valery ducked into the pool as they went off. They felt like they were next to a drum set. Once the fire died out, they came back up and bolted for the door. They slammed their bodies into it as it started to open more. A Valkyrie got its head, leg and an arm stuck in in the entrance. Lydia woke up gasping, "What the fuck?"

"Get me a fucking gun!" Calvin shouted as the operative tried pushing the door open. The captured alien screamed for help. Lydia asked, "What?"

"Give me a fucking gun already!" He shouted louder as a drone came through the door. Hail joined in, slamming the door shut. The Valkyrie got her foot crushed.

A drone that was crushed in half aimed a pistol at Calvin's head. It had its head crushed with a rifle stock. Zen gasped after hitting it one last time. Calvin shouted at her, "Get armored up!"

"What?" she asked again as the others crawled up from the pool and started donning their suits, not even bothering to clean themselves first. Audie snapped, "Getting killed sucks!"

"No shit!" Zen shouted at him as there was a thump on the door. Calvin quickly shouted, "Duck!"

All of them went back into the pool as the door burst open with fire following close behind. Before the fumes could die down, Hail and Zen were leaping back out of the pool and firing grenades into the passageway. A group of drones tried to sacrifice themselves to save the wounded Valkyrie operative. Their metal bodies weren't enough as they were ripped to bits. Another operative charged in firing away. Valery grabbed her and pulled her into the pool. Zen then used a jagged fragment and stabbed the Xenos in her throat repeatedly. She only stopped when the alien was dead and sinking like a brick to the bottom. Lydia and Audie popped out of the pool and finished off the surviving machines. The fire team scrambled to get their armored suits back on as soon as possible. They didn't bother to clean the blood and gunk off themselves. Calvin was the last one to get his suit on as everyone else was holding the line. Several auto turrets came down the passageway, helping push back the drones. All six of them threw grenades at the pack of machines. The electro bursts caused them to burst open from the inside out. The onslaught caused the drones to pull back but not before destroying another two turrets. Audie shouted, "Our auto turrets suck! Also, why don't we use drones?"

"Drones aren't fucking loyal!" Lydia shouted, holding down the trigger to her weapon, letting plasma fly from the rifle and shooting another four machines. Valery sighed, "As fun as a last stand is, how are only seven of us supposed to fend off these fucks?"

"Killing them faster than they can kill us!" Calvin shouted as five more drones got cut down as they tried to move forward. Their dead shells were now blown apart, staining the walls with oil and hydraulic fluid. Things calmed down for a second as the machines pulled back. Calvin was about to charge after them when Hail stopped him, "Wait a second old man; you're on your seventh life. You could go insane soon if you take anymore abuse. Hold the fort down with Valery while we push ahead."

"What?" Calvin asked him in dismay as he saw the hallucination of Helena again. "You should listen to you son," she said.

"You're right. Start pushing them back to the airlock. We'll at least give you cover," Calvin agreed as Hail nodded, "Don't worry about a thing. We got this."

"Right," Lydia scoffed in dread, double checking her weapons and gear. The others did the same, not looking forward to having to push ahead. Calvin told them, "Don't let your number get too high. It's bad for your health."

"You fuckers owe us!" Audie told him as the five of them started down the passageway together. Valery sighed, "Those are some good kids, aren't they?"

Their hallucination started talking to them, "So brave. Would you have brought them into this world if you knew what they were in for?"

"I didn't have a choice. Well… maybe I did… I was lonely," Calvin told her as he made sure he wasn't being listened to in vain. Doc sighed, "The two of you have some major screws loss."

"Shut up!" Valery shouted at him. Calvin scoffed, "You picked a hell of a time to show back up."

"What part of me representing your resolve don't you understand?" she told him while looking around the lab, "This place is a mess. Bet you're going to be on the cleaning party."

"You're killing my motivation to live! Besides,

one thing at a time my dear," he told her gesturing with his finger. Valery laughed, "You sick masturbator."

"You know you like it!" he told her as they both laughed for a second. They looked in the direction of a firefight occurring nearby. Part of him wanted to bolt towards the action. Yet feeling the hands of an imaginary friend reminded him of his fragility. He flinched with every illumination of the dark passageway. Calvin sighed, "Come on guys. You got this!"

"Thanks!" Audie said popping out of the pool. Lydia was close behind him, "Asshole!"

They both quickly got into their armored suits and back into the fight, leaving Calvin and Valery alone with their dark thoughts again. He grumbled, "I can't just stand back and do nothing!"

"We'll get our chance," Valery told him as Helena laughed, "You two are so lucky to have each other."

Hail and Zen popped out from the pool. Zen screamed, "Those cheap bastards!"

They both got armored suits on. Calvin went up to Hail, "What's going on?"

"Good news is that they're running out of robots. Bad news is that those dwarves are tough," Hail told him before charging forward once more with Zen in tow. Helena nodded, "You wouldn't think such an alien race would be so strong, would you?"

"I know you're a figment of my imagination but shut up!" Valery shouted at her. Barbra popped up, "Don't go insane yet!"

"Too late for that. How goes the battle?" he asked her, quickly wanting to change the subject. She sighed, "Haven't lost the ship yet."

She got armored up and went back into the fight. Helena told him, "You don't deserve them."

"Why would I think that? Because I'm a terrible person or because I doomed them?" he wondered out loud. Valery sighed, "What is with this bitch?"

"Another damned test. We're still here Holly!"
Calvin shouted in frustration as the Doctor sighed, "You're
just going crazy."

All five of the others came popping out of the pool.
Hail laughed, "We got them on the ropes!"

"You all just got wasted," Calvin pointed out as the
got armored up again. Lydia told him, "So are they.
They're running out of tin cans to throw at us. We're
starting to see more of their ship's reaction force coming
on board, too."

Barbra went up to him, "You two want to join us
for the next round?"

"Hell yeah!" Valery shouted, as Calvin nodded,
"You know I do."

The seven of them went back down the
passageway, pushing past the destroyed machines, dead
bodies and destroyed turrets. The debris bounced off their
suits as they went along. Nothing seemed to be in one piece
from all the rounds and explosives going off. Zen asked,
"Should we check to make sure the vital areas of the ship
are good or go on the offensive?"

"Let's be offensive," Calvin told her as Valery
added, "Always be offensive!"

Barbra laughed, "Oh the puns."

"I'm not sorry for being so offensive," he told her
as they moved forward. Two drones flew towards them
from around the corner. Lydia and Audie quickly shot
them in the head multiple times. Calvin and Barbra threw
grenades that bounced off the corner and down the next
area. Hail and Zen boosted ahead laying down cover fire
for them to move up. The machines were starting to pull
back. The team didn't let up the chase, firing away
whenever they popped up in their sights. Soon they're back
to where they started. The bulkheads were all charred
black, and there was a wall of parts and bodies drifting
around. They fired off a couple shots at anything still
moving. Zen laughed, "All clear in here!"

"Let's kill them!" Calvin shouted. They started planting as many explosives as would fit on a broken metal board and pointed it forward towards the beach point. They pushed it forward. When the Valkyries tried to attack them, they used an energy shield, detonating the explosive. The metal board focused the blast toward the entry point, either killing or disorienting those in the line of the blast. Calvin shouted, "Breach!"

Calvin led the charge forward with everyone else following him. He used both his side arm and rifle to shoot the two enemy auto turrets into scrap. He shouted, "Don't let those fuckers escape!"

"That's the spirit!" Barbra shouted as she and the others stormed into the enemy vessel. The drones were now fewer in number, coming at them in piecemeal. He laughed, "They're spent! For..."

Chapter 11
Piracy
2273
Orbit of Earth
Pandora
Resurrection Bay

ALVIN suddenly woke back up in the pool of muck and slime. He quickly pulled himself out, gasping, shivering and still in shock. Valery was standing over him, "That was inspirational, until you took a round to the head."

He looked down at his wrist now saying 8A on it. He grumbled, "Shit! It's almost up to double digits now."

"Yep, that sucks," she told him sympathetically. Calvin tried to stand up but was unable to maintain his balance. Valery grabbed him. He gasped, seeing she had the same number. "We're in this together."

He smiled at her as they got armored up again. They headed back out into the passageway. There were crewmembers and Marines running around the ship this time. Valery laughed, "About time we got fucking back up!"

"Sorry we're late!" one of them shouted as they secured the Pandora. The mess left behind by the destroyed machines was being gathered up and disposed of along with the dead bodies. There was a long trail of carnage as the two of them made their way back to the hanger bay. When they got there, they saw all the Titans and ground crews firing at the breach in the door, keeping the drones at bay. They all took turns firing so none of their weapons would overheat. One of the Titans was firing off rocket rounds that exploded when they got out into space. These models looked identical to the ones they used earlier with two sets of cannons in the torso, boosters on multiple places on the legs, blue colored armor all over the humanoid figure, a set of cannons on the round head, and a jet customized for space combat. There were two that were available for them to use. Valery smiled, "Thinking what I'm thinking?"

"Mount up."

"Don't need to tell me twice," Valery told him itching to fly one of those Mechs again. Calvin joked, "Race you."

"You're on." They both rocketed across the bay as the battle raged, dodging rounds as they came in. The hatches opened for them, and they both rushed to hop inside. Valery laughed, "I win!"

"Let's see who can get the most kills," he told her, getting his machine ready as it came to life. Both had their machines dual wield a cannon that looked like a machine gun and a rocket launcher. They moved towards the breach as four transports got loaded up with the personnel that were available. The other Titans moved forward, keeping up the fire. Holly came on the net, "Great job on being bait. Now let's finish taking this ship for ourselves."

"You are being surprisingly honest for once," he told her as the doors opened in front of them. Holly scoffed, "When haven't I been?"

"You drugged us multiple times," Valery pointed out as three enemy Mech appeared in front of them and were shot to pieces before they could react. Calvin and Valery launched out into space with the four transports and six other Titans following them. It was chaos outside and the Diamond shaped Valkyrie ships were now getting swarmed by multiple smaller Consortium Tri-Star shaped destroyers popping out of the void. It was like seeing a pack of wolves attacking a polar bear. The Pandora looked well for being at the bottom of a bay for decades. They held on to the Valkyrie vessel for dear life as it tried getting away from them. There were multiple connections keeping the two vessels together. Both sides were sending what seemed to be a never-ending stream of meat and metal into the fray. The eight Titans and four transports headed right toward one of the hangers of the Valkyrie ship. The Pandora gave what cover fire she could as they headed in. The Titans fired off multiple decoys as laser rounds came flying at them. One of them destroyed a Mech that couldn't maneuver in time. Another cut a transport in half with the personnel inside flying out into space as the ship disintegrated. Despite the flack they were getting, they were closing in on the doors. Calvin flew right to one of the cracks where two doors met up. The Titans used their heavy launchers to fire a salvo of plasma rockets, blasting a breach in the door. From the breach came a volley of fire that took out another Titan, vanishing in a flurry of light. They all went flying from the shield as it impacted into the hull. One of the transports took several hits but pushed its engines and crashed through the opening. Calvin and Valery fired into the breach giving cover fire to the first wave. The other four Titans pulled the doors open further allowing the other two to land inside. The drones and Valkyrie operatives started pulling back into the vessel as their defenses faltered. Valery and Calvin flew in blasting away at anything that stood in front of them. The personnel pushed ahead and started heading into the ship. One of the Titans was shot from behind as another squadron challenged them. Calvin and Valery turned around and fired back. The drones were quickly disposed of, faltering to the fire. The piloted machine managed to take out one more Titan before fighting Calvin and Valery. They both pulled out their melee weapons, blocking the sticks from the machine. The enemy Titan looked like diamonds formed together to create a humanoid figure. It repeatedly jabbed at them pushing them into the bay. One of the feet of the machine smashed a transport as they went further inside. One advantage their Titans had was built-in weapons. As the sticks came at them, they'd take pot shots, whittling away at the machine's armor. The head suddenly started to glow and fired an energy round at them. They dodged the blast and stabbed the machine in the torso and head. Valery shouted, "Fuck yeah!"

"That's the way it's done!" Calvin shouted. The hanger seemed secure. Outside, the Valkyrie fleet seemed to be getting subdued as each of them were boarded. A couple managed to self-destruct rather than get taken over. Most however fell to the borders. Valery had her Titan pat Calvin on the shoulder, "It's good to win for once!"

"Good to be..." Calvin paused seeing a Valkyrie machine come to life next to them and made a lunging motion towards Valery with a large plasma sword. Calvin moved forward with his Titan taking the stabbing right in the torso. As the hot blade went up towards the cockpit, every weapon on the Titan fired away, blasting apart the enemy machine. He suddenly felt hot as everything around him started to burn. He laughed, "Not such a bad person now am..."

CHAPTER 12
RESURRECTIONS
2274
ORBIT OF MARS
C.S.W. JASON
RESURRECTION BAY

CALVIN came crawling out of the muck again, screaming as he still felt like he was on fire. His vision was blurry as he tried to look around. He saw a figure standing in front of him, "Took you a while this time. Still holding on?"

He tried to get a better look at her, hesitating as he didn't know if she was a figment of his imagination or not. Then Helena told him, "Say yes."

"Yeah. Still hanging in there. How long was I out?" he asked her as he crawled out of the pool, stumbling to his knees. The pain wasn't subsiding fast enough for him. Holly lowered her pistol and offered him a syringe. He quickly injected himself with it feeling better immediately. She sighed and handed him a towel, "You're going to develop an addiction if you take too much of that stuff."

"I really don't think that my situation could possibly get any worse than it already is... wait! I take it back!" Calvin told them, unable to do so as the others laughed. Holly replied smiling, "Even you know that things can always get worse. Also, thanks for delivering my message. Got approval and a goodbye from my father. May he rest well."

"Any time that you slip something past me..."

Calvin started as he realized that happened to him way too often. "Why do I do this to myself?"

Holly smiled, "Because it's better to burnout than to fade away."

"One way of looking at it," he told her with sickening mix of genuine glee, pride, and joy. Calvin was slack jawed by this and his situation in general. He grumbled, "My fire team?"

"They're fine. Glad you thought of them for once," Holly told him mockingly. Calvin rolled his eyes, "Everyone is a critic."

"I'm sure they'll understand if you're late like your last two kids did," Holly added insult to injury. Calvin snapped and managed to upper cut Holly in the jaw, then slammed her onto the deck, choking her, "Fuck you! You knew! You set me up!"

"Harder daddy!" She shouted with seeming glee. Calvin snapped the pistol out of her hands and kept choking. She weakly laughed, "Where was this ferocity the other night?"

"Fuck you!" He shouted at her as she rasped, "Yes...!"

Calvin ripped her coverall open, showing off her body again. He pushed down into her, "This what you wanted you psycho!"

"Stop being a bitch!" She shouted at him slapping him across the face as he thrust downward with as much force as he could, "Fuck!"

"I hate you!" He yelled at her as he kept moving. He wanted to be as violent as possible, putting as much force into it as he could. Adding an insult, "Your father died a sad pathetic artificial intelligence!"

"Yes!" She gasped with pleasure despite the abuse. Calvin tried again, "He got stuck with bad variables!"

"Oh yeah!" She gasped as he gyrated as fast as he could, trying to hurt her. It had the opposite effect. He tried going faster, yet it only added to their sensations. "Oh, damn it!"

Both climaxed at the same time and went limp on top of one another. As they gasped, Holly told him, "You are a horrible person. Just accept it and maybe today you won't be an asshole."

Calvin got up and started walking away, "Guess it takes one to know one psychotic bitch!"

"See you for dinner?"

Calvin left the bay, tracking a trail of slime where he stepped. He ignored the crewmen shouting at him as he made a mess through the passageways. One of them got in his way and he punched him in the face hard enough to send them flying into a bulkhead, knocking him out cold. He punched another two crewmen before everyone got the hint to get away from him. Calvin walked back into the Chief's berthing and went right into the showers. After turning on one and climbing inside, he collapsed to the deck screaming his lungs out and bursting into tears, punching dents in the metal bulkheads. After a minute of this he sat in the shower, letting the water run. Valery sighed, "Drink?"

He looked down seeing her once more drugged up on the shower's deck, "Fuck it."

He grabbed the bottle and took a long swig. "Thanks for saving me. You fucked Holly again, didn't you?"

"Yes," he told her, taking another swig of the drink. He took a couple deep breaths and wiped the tears from his eyes. Valery started to pass out in a pool of her own vomit. He reached over and tapped her as she sat up and spit everything out of her mouth, rinsing it soon afterwards. As she got herself together, Calvin asked, "You, okay?"

"Are any of us?" she replied still spitting into the deck drain. She then took several pills and showed them off on her tongue. Calvin grumbled, "Sloppy seconds time?"

"Don't remind me." she told him still with her

tongue out as he used his teeth to get the pills for himself. He felt intoxicated in seconds with any reservation or shame vanishing as the drugs kicked in. Then he pushed Valery against the wall while rubbing their tongues together. Calvin pushed down into her as she scratched his back gasping. The water drenched them adding to the heat as they slammed into each other, desperate to feel. She gasped, "You got stamina!"

"You two sick fucks masturbating again?" Rotten asked from outside. Calvin threw the bottle making him back away, "Watch me do me!"

"Oh yeah!" Valery shouted as he leaned down kissing her again. Lane then shouted, "You're both disgusting!"

"Worth it!" Calvin shouted as they climaxed in the shower. They held still for several seconds, feeling numb all over. Calvin sat next to Valery sighing, "Did we just do that for the third time?"

"Our clones are going to hate us," she sighed, still gasping. Calvin nodded, "Was the camera saved?"

"Yeah. Sturdy thing. Hail is waiting on us. Are you going to be able to handle it?" she asked him still gasping. He looked over at her, "As long as I'm not alone."

"You do know this relationship is bad right? Masturbation isn't a relationship." she told him plainly. He laughed, "Beats Holly."

CHAPTER 13
DEPRESSION AND LIQUOR
2274
ORBIT OF MARS
C.S.W. JASON
MESS DECKS

SURE, you want to watch this?" Hail asked as they patched the camera into the projector. Hail, Zen, Lane, Rotten, and Valery had the mess decks to themselves. Calvin took a long drink, "No, but we need to know what happened. At least I'm not sober."

"The cranks would hate it if you destroyed the mess decks. Also, Sophia offered you a chance to join the interrogation afterwards on the little twerp," Rotten informed him. Valery asked, "How was Earth for you all?"

"We found an empty tomb like you. Just no Pandora or... recordings." Lane told her as she looked back, "Why is Zen here?"

"She asked me. May we get started?" Hail replied. Calvin nodded, "Play."

The projector showed the recordings being accessed. They went to the first video. It showed people they knew celebrating at a formal place. The date read 2022, 10-year anniversary of the victory. People they knew were getting drunk. Most of them were in dress uniforms, others in brightly colored formal attire. Yeager was one of them laughing, "Ten years and many more!"

"How about ten more drinks!" Connor McCormick shouted as he fell, taking a table with him. Mira laughed at him while pointing at a statue next to him, "Lightweight!"

"You'd think they'd learn how to do a marathon and not a sprint. What's with the camera? Never knew you were a hipster," Vera smiled into the device. Yeager laughed, "Fuck off! This is a top-of-the-line relic right here! Also, it was a gift from my mother."

"Thought that counts," she told him as Alec Dumont walked in, "I might need that later so I can become a star."

"You already are one, old geezer," Yeager joked with him as both finished their drinks. Alec sighted, "Come on, I'm not that old!"

Calvin sighed, "That motherfucker."

"Don't let bitterness get the better of you," Valery told him as they kept watching. A Commander with Doctor Murphy behind him was giving a speech about how things have gotten better, and they were now going to establish colonies in another system. After the speech was over, Alec commented, "Thought the new boss was going to be the same as the old one but guess not. Things can change for the better. Revolution worked for once!"

"We made it work," Jane told them. Alec laughed, "If it isn't my favorite number."

"Mine, too," she told him as they kissed. Calvin couldn't help but feel a bit of envy and anger seeing them together, knowing they both played him. Valery sighed, "Hope he enjoyed your sloppy seconds. Am I right?"

"I guess," Calvin sighed, trying not to let his dismay get the better of him. Rotten patted his shoulder, "You have Valery. Not enough?"

They both looked back at him as he backed off holding his hands up. Hail sighed, "I need a therapist."

"So do I," Zen joked with him. Calvin remembered the video where they were rubbing his poor fate in his face. Despite that, he kept his cool not flipping his lid this time. Might be because he could guess their endings. Part of him wanted to see them suffer. Vera laughed, "You're only here to get tomorrow off."

"It's why most of us are here. Time off to party off!" Alec slurred his words. Yeager joked, "You're not much of a poet. You should stick to your day job."

"You're a day job." he told him jokingly as Vera laughed, "That doesn't make any sense."

The recording ended with Alec passing out and the others drawing on his face. The next several files were photos of the day after with Alec covered in graffiti. Mira and Connor both took turns on the toilet vomiting while flipping the camera the bird. Next photos were of Yeager traveling, flying old Mechs, going on dates with a woman, and then led up to the decommissioning of the Pandora one year later. The next film was in New Seattle showing the construction of the new top layer. They're on the bay sailing towards the city. Yeager commented "Mega cities are a sight. Aren't they, honey?"

"I like the plans of Mars better, but this isn't bad," she told him. She was slender with black hair, pale skin, wide brown eyes, and rose lips. She looked over at the camera operator, "Letting Vera fool around with your obsolete camera? Thought you liked that thing."

"It has charm. No need to call it obsolete," he told her as Vera sighed, "What's that supposed to mean?"

"You break stuff constantly," she told her as she laughed, "That only happened maybe three times... okay four. I said I was sorry about the car."

"You should be," she told her. Calvin was amazed to see Yeager not angry or being abrasive for once. Yet again, he resented him to the end. Yeager got on his knee in front of the woman, "Will you marry me, Laity?"

She giggled with joy as she accepted the ring from him, "Bravo brother!"

"I always could count you to capture the right moments," he told Vera as she cheered them on. Laity told him, "I have news, too. I'm pregnant."

Yeager smiled, "I'm going to be a father?"

Calvin paused the video groaning to himself. "Oh, come on! Come on!"

"Pausing it isn't going to change anything," Lane told him while patting his shoulder. Valery sighed, "Why are we doing this to ourselves? We know this isn't going to turn out well. Holly must have known about this recording. She's playing us."

"I don't know... not like we owe them anything... But they were the last ones standing," Calvin told her, feeling conflicted. Hail came up with, "They left that camera in hopes someone would watch it. Why not us?"

With that being said, Rotten pushed play again and they let the video keep going. Yeager was hugging Laity. Both were smiling and happy. He sighed, "Today it's a shame they're putting the Pandora out to pasture. End for one is a beginning of another."

"God that's corny!" Vera told him as he laughed, "Oh, lighten up!"

Kathryn came into the picture and hugged both Yeager and his new fiancé Laity. "I'm so happy! I'm going to be a grandmother! I'm old."

"Don't look a day above 42," Vera joked. Kathryn scoffed, "Not all of us can be a baby like you."

"I'm 11!" She told her jokingly, knowing it was a young age. She'd also gotten her aging sped up, "So, told them about your recruiting duty yet?"

"Why would you do that to yourself?" Laity asked him. As he was about to explain, they got interrupted. Vera, Yeager, and Kathryn got emergency calls. "Something's going on."

"Get the boat ashore now! We need... what the..." Yeager paused as they looked up. The sun flashed blue before the video stopped.

The recording stopped. Everyone could figure out what happened next. Hail sighed, "Damned bomb, right?"

"Yeah. Camera being more primitive helped it survive," Lane said knowing what was to come wouldn't be good. Valery sighed, "I'm not into misery porn."

"Neither am I," Calvin told her, pushing on. There were multiple photos of the city falling apart as power shut down all over. It showed them trying to figure out how to bring it back online in vain. They at least got the reactors stable so they wouldn't blow up. Then photos popped up of the environment dying bit by bit. Because most of Earth's environmental controls were artificial, it wouldn't last without the power system. Calvin pushed the play button, starting the next recording. It was a birthday for a small child. Everyone looked haggard and were in drab clothing with ripped off pieces from armored suits strapped onto them. In the background were tracked tanks, old brass projectile weapons and gear straight out of the twentieth century. A primitive generator kept the lights illuminating the event. They decorated the fox hole with what they had. The temperature looked like it was dropping as their breath could be seen. Yeager told his son, "Blow out the candle!"

One thing stuck out. Laity wasn't in the recording. Calvin quickly checked one of the photos and saw a white cross with her name on it. "Oh…"

"She wasn't meant to give live birth," Valery pointed out as Rotten added, "She chose to give him a chance at life in exchange for her own."

"You're going to make me cry," Lane said cracking up. The recording carried on with cheers as the child blew out the candle on the small cake. He let out a little, "Yeah!"

"Hope you made a good wish. Let's get you a slice, Steven!" Yeager told him as the started cutting the cake. Vera joked, "Save some for the rest of us."

"Don't worry… there's…. enough," he told her, trying to not point out the painfully apparent. Valery told him, "Your mother made the right call getting this camera. It's a tank."

"I remember telling you it had charm. Surviving is

a charm we all need right now." He gave his slice to his son as he happily took bites of the sweet treat. Calvin sighed heavily, feeling a knot in his throat, "I was a grandfather?"

"Fuck," Valery rubbed the top of her head. Rotten and Lane both gave supportive pats on their shoulders. Kathryn presented a gift to the small child. It was a helmet, "This will keep you safe from falling objects."

Connor gave him a coat, "This will keep you warm."

Mira handed him a toy gun, "You'll need to learn how to use this."

Yeager looked up at her in dismay as she stared at him back as if she were wanting to say, "You know it's true."

Jane walked up, "I'm out doing all of you! Spartan action figure!"

"How did you get that?" Yeager asked in amazement, handing the figure to the happy child. His smile broadened as he held the figure. Jane laughed, "One's person's... not gift is another person's treasure."

Yeager smirked at her wording. Steven laughed pointing at the figure, "Daddy!"

"Yeah... I had a suit like that once." Yeager said almost letting his anguish out. Alec came running into the picture, "Sorry, they're coming!"

Yeager sighed, "Really? I'll be back as soon as I can, buddy."

He put his helmet on and joined the others as they rushed to the front. Vera followed them forgetting to turn it off. She checked her old weapon to make sure it was ready, "We had a truce!"

"They're the ones that are breaking it," Alec shouted as an artillery shell landed near them. Mira sighed, "I miss my power armor."

Conner sighed, "We all do. Make do."

"Why can't we just negotiate again?" Jane asked.

Kathryn pointed out, "Probably because we're all running out of food. Now focus."

Several former Spartans were manning up a trench line as a wave of others came charging at them. It was something out of ancient times as they fired at one another. Only head shots would get a confirmed kill. Jane shouted, "Vera, turn off that damned camera!"

"Shit, my bad."

The recording stopped. The saw there were about five more recordings left with photos filling the gap of each one of them. The pictures showed the aftermath of the battle. Everyone was bewildered. Soon after, they did what they could to get ready for the next round of fighting. There were a couple more fights shown with group photos following soon after. Their numbers were dwindling along with their resources. Disturbingly, Steven stopped showing up in photographs. They checked and saw the last one was Kathryn holding the new 2-year-old in her arms waving at the camera. There was an artillery shell coming down behind them in the photo. Two crosses were shown with their names on them. Everyone started drinking heavily. Valery gasped, "Fuck!"

"I'm really starting to hate these damned Aliens," Rotten said. Lane sighed, "Maybe we should take up Sophia on her offer."

"Keep going," Calvin begrudgingly started the next one. "Three, two, one, Happy New Year!"

There were cheers throughout the group that looked even more haggard than before. Their uniforms looked patched together, weapons showed signs of wear, and gear looked beaten. All the men now had beards and the women had ragged hair that looked like it got cut with a knife. Mira laughed, "Another year and we live!"

"Still alive," Yeager said. He had a smile on, but he was clearly depressed. His eyes were sunken, hair was turning gray, and skin looked burnt. No one else was looking any better. Alec walked up to Yeager giving him a cigar, "Found these. Smoke them while we got them. Right?"

"Right." He lights them up taking a puff, then shared them with the others. Jane sighed, "Those might be the last ones… fuck. My bad."

"There's still hope. We're leaving the surface and heading up. We can get to the top and activate a beacon to get assistance from our old allies. We helped them out. They owe us a favor," Alec told them. Connor sighed, "Sure about that? If we could get jacked up like this, think they'll risk themselves by sticking their necks out for us?"

"It's something to try. Have anything else better to do?" Alec tried to maintain his calm but was breaking. Mira sighed, "Drink them while you got them, too. Last of the booze here at least."

"I know things are rough right now. We don't have our Doc to save us, but we don't need him. We'll have a chance when we're on top," Alec told them trying to convince himself as much as everyone else. The others in the background were loading up trucks with what gear and supplies they had left. Vera sighed, adding her support to him, "We'll have one hell of a view up there! Looking forward to seeing it."

"Incoming!" a voice shouted as an artillery shell landed nearby. The Camera fell to the ground as everyone grabbed their guns and opened fire on their attackers. Conner shouted, "Sticks and stones my ass, Einstein!"

He suddenly went backwards with blood coming out of his head. Mira screamed and charged up the trench, enraged as the camera was picked up and turned off. Calvin and Valery were starting to drink heavier the further along they went. The photos showed a funeral for Connor with Mira weeping over his body as he was covered in dirt. The cross had her name added to it in the next photo. There was a collective sympathetic gasp from everyone as they figured out what happened. Calvin commented "They went out together."

"Only a few more left," Valery told him as they went on. It showed their journey to the elevators. The vehicles either broke down or were blown up. Only a couple were left by the time the next video was recorded. They were all on a giant elevator nearing the next level. There were a couple others, but the focus was on Vera, Alec, Yeager and Jane. They looked worse than before with long air, dirty faces, thin bodies, and worn-out clothing. Their armored plating looked cheaply patched up with welds extending their lives. Vera commented as they looked east at the mountains while going up, "That is a hell of a view."

"Nothing like a good sunrise is there?" Yeager said trying to be sincere but coming off as sarcastic. He rephrased himself, "It's nice."

"Do you want to take some photos? Been using this more than you," Vera asked him as he sighed, "You keep it. You take great pictures."

"Thanks," she told him, taking it at face value. She must have known that it reminded him of his lost mother, wife and child. Alec sighed, "Making great progress. When we get to the top, we'll smoke the good stuff!"

He showed them four large rolled up joints. The others laughed with glee at seeing them. "Hell yeah!"

"They'll work better with the thinner air up there!" Jane pointed out as they laughed. Alec reminded her, "Remember, save them for later."

"We can join the mile-high club!" Jane told Alec as he sighed, "We've been higher than that."

"Use the truck!" Vera shouted at them. They did so as the others kept looking at the rising sun. The city was in its death throes below with multiple fires going and gun fights that could be heard from up there. Yeager sighed, "They're killing us without firing a shot."

"We'll survive this and give them what for," Vera told him patting him on the shoulder. He nodded, "Yeah. Karmas got to work for once."

The lift suddenly rocked as it malfunctioned. The camera dropped again. Vera managed to save it. Yeager grabbed on as he tried to stop the lift. The last of the vehicles started tumbling over the side. Alec was thrown out by Jane at the last second before it went over, "No!"

Calvin and Valery gasped, "Fuck!"

"I'm feeling bad for these people, even though they screwed us. Is that weird?" Rotten asked as Lane sighed, "It's human."

A part of Calvin felt this was karma for leaving him to die. The other part felt like they deserved better than what they were given, especially Yeager, "I thought I was unlucky. Damn me for complaining."

"We were probably avoiding becoming zombie food when this happened," Valery pointed out. Rotten scoffed, "Oh just have some damned sympathy."

"Next one." Lane pushed them on.

No one pushed the button for a minute as they sat there staring at the camera. Hail brought up the next photos. This time there were multiple photos of random things: streets, art, abandoned vehicles. It was like Vera was trying to get as many photos as possible. There were only six left in their group at this point. Then the next recording started. Alec commented, "Those doesn't look like Stallion ships."

"At least they're not Vegan. Think this is payback for betraying them?" Vera asked as Yeager scoffed, "Can't betray someone when we're never loyal to them."

"Yeah..." Vera said holding something back. Yeager started to lose it. "What?"

"Nothing. I think we should keep paying attention to the ship... incoming!" She shouted as they all ducked down. One of their fellow travelers was shot multiple times. The other five rushed for cover as another one of them was shot. The third person shot at the droids with no effect. She was then shot. Yeager shouted, "Damn it! This is crap!"

"Buddy, I got a confession. The beacon isn't a sure thing," Alec told him as he grabbed what grenades he had left forming a plan. "What? That's our only shot!"

The building they were in came under fire by the droids. Alec sighed, "It is a shot, but honestly I can't vouch for it. Even if it does work, well..." Alec pauses as they looked at the droids closing in around them. "I'll distract those fuckers for a bit. The elevator can go up one of two ways. One is to a resort that has booze, a view and history. The other is the area we were originally going for. Good luck."

Yeager tried to stop him, but he ran out throwing a grenade, destroying one of the bots. He successfully led most of them away from Vera and Yeager as they fled the area. The recording stopped. Calvin shed a single tear, "Got one last punch in on me, Alec."

Valery refilled his drink. There was a photo of memorial for Alec. Zen sighed, "Rest in peace."

Valery pushed play on the second to last video. It was just Yeager and Vera playing in the snow with vodka bottles. They made their choice to go to the resort instead of the array. Both looked happy being on the top of the structure. Calvin and Valery shed more tears at the sight of them having fun in the twilight of Earth, man, and their lives. The moment lasted for several minutes as the sun started to set. The recording ended with just one more video left. Calvin pushed play. It was Vera holding the camera up with Yeager curled up next to her. They were smoking the joints given to them earlier. "Well, we're going to sleep soon. It's cold outside. Hope someone sees this and knows we lived and enjoyed our rearranging of the place. No one to stop us from moving the museum around. We ate the last of our rations, drank all the booze and finally got to smoke those joints. Alec wasn't kidding about the booze. It's making me feel sleepy. He really hooked us up one last time, didn't he?"

Yeager nodded, smoking away as fast as he could

while savoring the smoke. Vera smiled, "I know this is a longshot. Dad, if you find this, I'd like you to remember me being happy."

"I'm sorry I threw you under the bus and never gave you a chance," Yeager told the recording, "I hung a painting next to the first one. Thought it was poetic."

"Don't be a downer. That's what the pills are for," she told him jokingly. "Shit! They found us!"

Camera dropped and there were sounds of a quick gun fight. Vera and Yeager went out swinging as they emptied their weapons before falling to the floor with burning holes in their heads.

"Goodbye," Calvin said choking up. Valery leaned next on him, and they hugged. Rotten, Lane, Zen and Hail moved around them, patting their shoulders in support. After a minute of letting their emotions out they all sat down at the same table and refilled their glasses with more booze. They drank quietly in the dimly lit mess deck. Calvin sighed, "Life well lived."

They all cheered. After that drink, Valery spoke, "Tough break for them."

"A bit cold hearted, don't you think?" Lane told her with a reply of, "We don't owe them shit! This isn't even our timeline and Holly probably had this sob story waiting for us so we'd do something stupid."

"You're probably right. I am going to do something stupid. I'm going to kill the shit out of these aliens." Calvin told them with his hands tighten into fists. "Why?"

"Someone has to. Besides, sounds more fun than just floating around this system." Calvin told her while looking her in the eyes with sincerity knowing this is what he wanted. Valery sighed, "You're going to regret that choice. I know it."

Calvin smiled, "Got enough of those as is. What's one more?"

CHAPTER 14
INDULGENCE AND WHAT NOT
2274
C.S.W. JASON
OFFICER'S QUARTERS

CALVIN woke up feeling drained. Thankfully, he had enough energy to run to the nearby toilet and vomit violently. His body hurt all over like he'd just gotten resurrected again. He checked his number and still saw 9A. He sighed, "Oh thank goodness."

"I wouldn't say that just yet," his hallucination told him, pointing at a bed. He looked back and his jaw dropped at the sight of Valery and Holly's naked bodies above the sheets, right next to each other. He realized what happened the night before right away, "Oh…"

"You dog you! Can't stop masturbating and screwing that lunatic, can you? You've done it three times already, sick bastard," Helena teased while laughing to herself. This time he wasn't fazed by waking up with them again. "Got laid. Why stress about it?"

"That video fucked you up, didn't it?" She asked him. Calvin struggled not to make a sound as he cleaned himself up the best he could. He sighed, "You know the answer to that."

"I also know Holly intentionally wanted you to find that camera." Helena told him. He looked back at her, "What?"

"Valery is right, and you know it. Holly wants to tie up loose ends. You're one of them. You already had a high number, and the Pandora's system was highly flawed

97

to say the least. You're eventually going to lose your mind," she warned him. Calvin scoffed, "Please, I'm already nuts for keeping this up as long as I have. At least I go out avenging someone."

"Someone who was never yours to avenge. Also, let me show you true insanity," she told him as he suddenly felt like he'd lost control of his body. It was moving around on its own incoherently. He screamed trying to take back control but was stuck as a passenger. When he did get back control, he dropped to the deck gasping, "Fuck!"

"That's what you're in for if you take the bait Holly gave you." she told him bluntly. "Why are you telling me this?" he asked.

"Self-preservation. I know you want vengeance. I don't think you'll find that if you go off once more." She then vanished in the dark. "You really are going mad, aren't you?"

Calvin looked over seeing Holly was awake. "That painfully apparent?" he replied.

"You mimicked the voice of someone long dead perfectly. I'd say you're off your rocker," she told him sitting up. "Hell of a thing knowing time is finite."

"You actually want to go on that mission?" she asked him, remembering what he'd just said. He nodded, "For once I do. I know what I'm getting into."

"I don't think so. I'd question your sincerity but seeing how you're already crazy enough to do a kamikaze... This is what I wanted. I'm honestly going to miss you," she told him. Calvin's eyes went up, "Really?"

"You're a good fuck, have the guts to stand up to me, and dependable. At least you'll be saving your son... brother... clones from the mission," she pointed out to him. He smiled, "Thanks for sweetening the deal. I'm sure you'll find someone to fill the void left by me well."

He gave her a wink. Holly struggled not to laugh. "I'm sure I will. Maybe I can see you off one last time."

"I wouldn't mind that. Got to go," he told her,

leaving the quarters. Calvin walked back to his berthing. This time everyone stayed away from him remembering his actions from the last time he went streaking. Helena laughed, "You're getting played. Where is your shame? Really have no modesty left?"

He ignored her as he walked into the darkened berthing. Lane and Rotten were sleeping together on the couch. Calvin let them sleep as he went into the shower and let the hot water come down on top of him, washing off his shame once more. He didn't know what was worse, that he was used to being a cog in the machine or that he wanted more. After sitting there for some time, he cleaned himself up and got dressed. Helena commented, "Think you'll get another promotion for your heroics?"

"Posthumous promotion," he joked with her. She sighed, "You're going to run out of uniforms with all the times you ditch them."

Calvin smiled, "Well spent."

"Cal, are you okay?" Rotten asked him. Calvin looked over seeing Lane and Rotten looking at him concerned, "Fine for now. Going to make the most of it while it lasts."

"Do you need to talk about the videos, Earth, anything?" Lane wondered. Calvin sighed as he got dressed, "No. I should let you all know that I'm going on the suicide mission."

"Why would you do that?" Rotten asked him, hopping out of his rack with Lane right next to him, "You're nuts."

"Not yet but getting there. It's fine. You'll have all of my clones to keep you company," he told them as they both cringed at the information. Rotten sighed, "You just managed to not get killed in a mission that was supposed to do that, and now you're going back for more? Why?"

"Why not? Better to go out in a blaze of glory than wither away. I can't let what happened on Earth go unanswered either." Calvin explained as Lane scoffed,

"Bullshit. You don't owe those people anything!"

"Not for them, for my own selfish need to keep fighting." Calvin tried to convey not convincing either one of them. "Holly is playing you. You really want to go along with what she wants? When has that ever worked out?"

"We're still here, aren't we?" He asked them as Lane grumbled, "You're a fuck boy for her, aren't you?"

"No, I'm not!" He shouted defensively. Rotten sighed, "Well, we'll see you off before the time comes. Clones won't be the same as you."

"Not coming?" Calvin asked them as they sighed, "No. We're good. One suicide mission was enough for us. Wish that was the case for you, too."

"Probably get replaced by replicates. We're staying here to rebuild," Lane told him. Calvin nodded, "Alright. Well, give my clones a chance. They'll be fine." As he left the berthing, he told them, "I'm getting ice cream."

"Save some for us," Rotten told him as Calvin gave them a nod.

As he went through the passageways, he took long looks at each part: the pipes, lights, emergency gear, and the blast doors. Jason was staying behind and he'd get sent back to the Pandora. Calvin laughed to himself thinking that was a fitting place to end. "Tough ship."

"Hey." A familiar voice came from behind him. He turned around to see his clone and Valery's standing there. Both were lower ranking and looked younger than him. "Hi. Good to see you two."

"Thanks..." Valery Clone said feeling puzzled. Calvin Prime laughed, "This whole universe is strange. Best to roll with it."

"You're the one that well... I can't judge." His clone tried to bring up his degeneracy but couldn't follow through. Calvin Prime sighed, "How many... siblings do you have?"

"Six that I know of. Four of them are on the mission," they said seemingly disgusted with the circumstances of their birth. Calvin nodded, "We're all here by accident. Don't feel bad about it. How much of my memories do we share?"

"Were you a street walker?" his clone asked him as they both laughed at the joke. Valery sighed, "I was."

They looked at her as she cracked up, "I'm kidding."

"Could have fooled us there," Clone Calvin joked as she playfully punched him. They laughed for a couple more seconds before his clone broke down and asked, "Yeah, how are you cool with this? We're abominations. Why would you do selfcest multiple times you sick bastard?"

Calvin told the truth, "Comfort. Just wanted to feel something other than fear and danger. Also, Valery was much kinder than Holly."

Calvin recognized what his clone was thinking. He added, "You may judge."

"Makes prison romance look clean." Valery's clone scoffed.

"That is actually a good analogy of our relationship." Calvin Prime explained as his clone sighed, "Please stop."

"Fair enough."

"You're really going off to avenge people that weren't yours to begin with?" His clone wondered. Calvin nodded, "Yes. Don't want to get stuck behind a desk. Also, I'm taking your spot."

"You can have it. Well, make those bastards pay," his clone told him as Calvin looked at Valery's clone figuring, "You're doing this because of Holly aren't you, boy toy?"

"You, too" he told her.

The two clones started walking off, "Hope you go out in a blaze of glory so I feel less ashamed about being myself."

"Sure thing." Calvin sighed feeling disgrace once more. "I am terrible."

Calvin made it to the mess deck again and got himself some rocky road ice cream. Valery walked in on him. He already had a cookies and cream bowl ready for her. She sat down in front of him. Both were able to realize by looking each other in the eyes that Valery was also going on the mission, too. "So, coming with me?"

"Killing ourselves in a suicide pact," she joked. They both sat there eating and enjoying the silence on the mess deck, focused more on the dessert in front of them than worrying about what was to come. Hail, Zen, and Barbra came walking in, "You two are predictable."

"Want to join us?" Calvin asked him. He sighed taking a set along with Barbra, "I could use some after last night."

"We drank heavily," Valery told her. Hail sighed, "I felt like we just met, and now I'm having to say goodbye... That's literally what's happening."

"Why are you two going on this mission?" Zen asked him as Calvin smiled, "Sounds like fun."

"Come on. Really? Even I know my mother is setting you up and Valery is just going out of loyalty to you." Hail told him, knowing there was something else. Calvin smiled, "We all should be so fortunate to choose when and where we go out. A chance to go out in a blaze of glory on my own accord is worth it. Best I can tell you."

"I bet you're not going to get what you want, old man. Well, make as many of those bitches hurt for what they did," Barbra told him while eating the ice cream. Lydia and Audie joined them. "Sounds like fun. We transfer to the Pandora in a few days, too."

"Dibs on middle rack." Audie told them. Hail looked over at them, "You two are going along as well?"

"Yeah. Voluntold. We should be running into your clones there, too," Lydia told him in an odd acceptance of their situation. Audie joked, "Must be nice being a mama's boy."

"I'll see if…" Hail got cut off by Calvin, "No."

"What, old man?" Hail asked in surprise. Calvin sighed, "We need experienced people in the home system. Guarding this place is just as important. Suicide mission is full, and you're not welcome to tag along this time."

Hail wanted to argue but knew he wouldn't be able to change things. "Guess I'll have to speculate on if this is a giant trap for you. Good luck then."

"Been lucky so far," Valery told him confidently. Calvin smiled, "What are you all going to do to live?"

Zen and Hail both looked at each other. Calvin sighed, "It's okay. You've got time to figure it out. And you'll have a good device to record it."

He handed Hail the camera. It was refurbished, looking brand new. His eyes went wide as he accepted the gift, "I'll record something worthwhile."

Zen giggled to herself. Valery gasped, "Aw. You two."

"When Earth gets healed, take a trip from the tip around the world. Lots to see and do," Calvin told them as they dug into the ice cream of their choice, sharing the silence as they indulged in the dessert. When they were done, Hail took a photo of them in the moment, "Life is good."

CHAPTER 15
PREMATURE FIGHT
2275
CONSORTIUM FLEET
C.S.W. PANDORA
ARMORY

"THOSE assholes only sent two hundred ships after us? I'm insulted. It should be at least a thousand," Valery joked as she got her armored suit on. All of them were getting rigged up to take abuse with plates and shielding being installed. Valery sighed as she checked over Calvin's set up. "It's two hundred and forty-three to be exact. For what it's worth, it's the thought that counts, especially seeing how they managed to react to us so quickly."

"Thoughts and hopes never seem to take us far, do they?" Lydia told her as they all started checking her suit. Audie held up one large plasma cannon with both hands and told them, "We're not dead yet, so we must be doing something right."

"Damn right!" Calvin patted him on the shoulder. Lydia sighed, "I miss Hail, Barbra, and Zen."

"What? I don't count?" Barbra's clone shouted. Hail's replicate sighed, "We're copies that don't count."

"You count to me," Calvin told them.

"Why worry about the ones left behind? They're the ones partying. See Zen and Hail's wedding? It looked fun," Audie mentioned wishing he were there. Calvin told him, "We'll have an even bigger party with gambling and prostitutes."

"Fuck yeah," Audie told him knowing it wouldn't happen, but he wanted to dream. So, did everyone else, "Fuck yeah!"

Hail sighed, "I hate being a replaceable commodity and not being an individual!"

The others looked at him, "Oh come on, I'm not the only one."

Barbara sighed, "Just don't think about it."

Valery told them, "Think about killing the aliens! Not going to be as easy. They're not going to make the same mistakes twice. Audie, is that going to fit in the cockpit?"

"I'll make it fit, ma'am," he told her as she nodded, "Right. Don't let it go off prematurely."

"Good with that," Barbra's clone scoffed as Audie shook his head. "Just not the same."

"Fuck you."

"How do we not have enough ships to rival them already? I thought the Dragon's Teeth was supposed to turn out ships like those old hot cakes. I heard those were quick to cook," Hail's clone asked her. Calvin chimed in, "That device wasn't able to crank shit out fast enough. They're saving most of the fleet to protect the home system. Only able to spare one hundred twenty-two ships. Give or take."

"At least we're doing our jobs as cannon fodder well," Lydia pointed out, taking a drink from a flask. Everyone was grabbing what weapons, ammo, and devices they could with what time they had left. Other teams were also gearing up. Hail sighed, "Look, we really need to have a conversation on how mom is sending me off to die while my original is living the high life. This is not okay!"

"She sent a copy of herself her, too. Nothing is sacred to her. Just thankful she let the others rest... I hope. You're a son to me for what it's worth," Calvin told him sympathetically. Hail sighed, "You're a patsy, old man."

Valery went on, "If there is one silver lining to this clusterfuck, the Valkyries have halted their advance against the Claws in order to kill us first."

"Claws are still in the fight despite their home system blowing up?" Audie pointed out. Valery sighed, "They're on the ropes."

"Another thing. Didn't we jam the communications between our system and theirs? How were they supposed to know that they had to send armada after us?" Lydia asked her as she was placing her helmet on. Calvin grumbled, "Things go wrong, that's life. Guessing they don't fuck around. Neither should we. Let's go!"

The team started to make their way to the hanger bay. There were crewmen and Marines running around to get to their stations. The air was being vented out and the gravity was on a timer to shut down. The lights were shutting off leaving them in the dark. The doors were also on a timer to close when the time came. Everyone had on some form of armored suit that would give them protection or at least a false sense thereof. Inside the hanger, the crews were working on getting the Mechs, fighters, and transports ready for launch. Anything that could fly was being sent out to fight. The Titans were standing by for them. Three had modified jet packs with a cannon over one shoulder and a rocket launcher over the other. The shields also had extra weapons built in to give an extra punch. They all started to mount up, hopping inside the giant machines and making them come back to life. Valery went on, "Our fleet is going to use holographic emitters to either go completely stealth or try to pass off as a Valkyrie ship. The vessel we took will help sell the illusion for a while. They won't buy it for long. We need to get in up close and personal. Understand?"

"Roger," Everyone replied. She added, "Don't forget, if the Pandora dies, we die, too."

"No pressure," Audie replied to her. Lydia

laughed, "That's the spirit."

Calvin got on a private link with Valery as the Titans got into their launch positions, "Are you good?"

"Are you? Don't worry about me. Keep the team and yourself in one piece." She told him. Calvin sighed, "Nothing is going according to plan."

"Really that much of a shocker?" she asked him. Calvin sighed, "Good point."

"All the more fun that we're winging it!" Hail shouted. Barbra laughed, "We're fucked."

Calvin got a camera feed and saw what they were up against, "Shit."

Their ships shimmered as they came into view. They ranged in size, but all looked like some form of diamond. In between them were thousands of fighters and Mechs flying in formation. The computer codenamed the machines, Harpies. Calvin couldn't help but feel that was a fitting name for them. The fighters looked like diamonds with wings attached. He moved his machine around as if he were limbering up for a sprint. Valery shouted, "Stand by!"

"Launch." Two by two they got catapulted out of the hanger and into space. They quickly got behind the Pandora as did all the others. Each one grabbed onto a transport to save energy and rode it like a board. Both fleets looked like two waves of vessels about to crash into one another. Calvin couldn't help but feel like an ant in the storm. Helena touched his shoulders, "Relax. You know how things will turn out eventually."

Oddly enough those words managed to calm him down. Valery told everyone, "Keep communications to a minimum until the fireworks show begins."

"Roger," everyone replied. Everything seemed to be too quiet as both fleets got closer to one another. Things were moving along quickly as they came within range. In an instant, both groups were firing on each other. Torpedoes, missiles, and plasma were flying between the two fleets. Vessels on both sides were being cracked open like a coconut being hit with a sledgehammer. The Pandora's weapons fired away with everything she had at a dreadnought that was twice her size. With concentrated bursts from multiple ships, the shields went down, the hull cracked, and a magazine was struck. She was taken out of the fight as multiple hull breaches burst open after the ordnance went off.

From the debris of the destroyed ship, the Valkyries sent forward all their fighters and Mechs. Valery told them, "Weapons free!"

They all opened fire. Each of them landed a hit as the enemy was packed together tightly. The swarm was cut to pieces by the explosions that showered the Harpies and fighters in molten plasma. The destroyers and frigates fired proximity rounds that animated whole squadrons of the enemy in flash. The Titans kept up a constricted rate of fire while the fighters started to flank the attackers. The transports acted as shields for the capital ships as they took hits for them. One Valkyrie ship flew up towards the Pandora sending a salvo of torpedoes at her. A frigate ended up sacrificing herself taking the hits. The beating caused the vessel to burst apart into nothing but small fragments. The debris flew all over the place hitting anything that got in the way. One of the Titans nearby got struck by a fragment and was crushed. The center of the Consortium fleet started to pull back. The Valkyrie fleet followed them giving chase. Any ship that had their engines taken out turned into a sitting duck waiting to get picked off. The Titans stuck with the Pandora as she fell back. Calvin shouted at them, "We just got orders: all the Titan squadrons will head into the enemy formations to slow them down."

"That sounds like fucking suicide!" Lydia shouted as the Valkyrie Harpies opened fire at them. Most of the Titans managed to dodge the blast. Three others were hit right in the torso, blowing up right way. Hail and Barbra fired proximity rounds that shredded four enemy machines upon detonation. Calvin laughed, "Every mission is a suicide mission for us! Isn't it awesome?"

"No, it's not!" Audie told him honestly.

"For Sol!" Valery pulled out a plasma saber and motioned for the Titans to follow her in a charge. All the machines rushed forward into the enemy formations, catching their Mechs and fighters by surprise. They didn't stand a chance as the Titans bashed their way through them. The thin harpies were crushed by the bulky Titans. The large capital ships didn't have time to fire their proximity rounds as the Mechs managed to get in close to them. The fighters snuck all the way around and were now striking the enemy fleet from behind. Their concentrated strikes crippled the giant enemy vessels. They did the same with their heavy weapons, all hitting a single weak point on the ship with everything they had. The capital ships took advantage of this by sending torpedoes into the breaches formed, finishing them off. The Valkyrie vessels tried to launch extra Harpies and fighters, but every time they did, the hangers would get targeted and blast apart. Out of desperation the Valkyrie ships started using the proximity rounds. They worked in taking out whole squadrons of Titans and fighters, but they also inflicted massive damage on their own vessels in the process. Calvin and his team banded together to avoid getting shredded by the flying fragments. As the fight went on, it was becoming apparent that the Consortium fleet was acting like fishing net with the Valkyries heading right into it. Calvin laughed, "We're pulling a Hannibal!"

"A what?" Lydia asked when from behind the Valkyrie fleet came Consortium reinforcements. They seemed to appear out of the void right behind the enemy. Every ship started to form a link between one another. Valery shouted, "Everyone, pull back to the Pandora!"

All the Consortium fighters and Titans started to fly as fast as they could out of the cluster of Valkyrie ships.

The Consortium fleet then pulled on the web with energy beams slicing apart anything it touched. The Valkyrie fleet was trapped. They ended up crashing into one another and trying to fire off everything they had to stave off the end. The Titans dodged the crashing vessels, pushing their engines to the limit. A squadron of Harpies chased after them, keeping up the fight. Valery broke off and headed towards them. Calvin shouted, "What are you doing?"

"Stalling for time. Now go!" She fired with every weapon she had taking down three of them. Calvin joined her, "You don't get to play hero by yourself!"

"Couldn't let me have my moment, could you?" Valery sighed as they both flew backwards and kept up the fire on the enemy machines. Both Titans pulled their sabers and clashed with the Harpies. Valery and Calvin competed with the other's maneuvers to see how many they could shoot down. As the machines fought one another, the fighting seemed to come to a stop when a nearby Valkyrie ship was cut to shreds with the debris flying around them. The Harpies all fled, trying to get away in vain. Valery sighed, "Good times always seem to end too soon."

Calvin tried to rush over to her. Her Titan looked over at him and waved. "Valery! Fly damn…"

CHAPTER 16
2275
ENDURANCE AND PAIN
SOL SYSTEM
C.S.W. JASON
RESURRECTION BAY

CALVIN screamed as he came out of the pool. His body felt like it was still under pressure from being crushed. He saw 10A on his arm now. "Shit."

A weapon was pointed at him, "Still sane?"

"Fuck off!" he shouted as another person came swimming up. Valery was crying. Calvin gasped, "No!'

The guard went over to her, "Still there, Val?"

"What was I thinking?" She mumbled looking around in a daze like she wasn't there. Calvin got to her, "Come on! Don't lose your shit now!"

"I went on this damned mission for you, Calvin! Selfish prick couldn't call it a day? One suicide mission not enough for you? Getting killed hurts," she told him feeling pain still from the last death. The guard lowered his weapon, "Good enough for me. Get out."

Valery didn't want to move, but both were yanked out of the pool and sprayed off. "What was I thinking?"

"Thank you for coming with me," Calvin told her as they got dried off. They left the bay and ventured into the ship. Calvin could tell that Valery needed a moment so found an empty fan room nearby and took her inside. He was about to kiss her when Valery stopped him, "I think we've done that too many times already."

"Why worry about doing it again? He asked as she scoffed, "I think our relationship is toxic. Not to mention this is wrong. All of it."

"Least toxic relationship I'm in right now. Look, I know getting killed sucks, but we both knew this would be it." Calvin tried to comfort her as she wept, "Weren't you listening? I came here because I didn't want to be alone. You're my only friend."

Calvin told her, "Even loners have at least two friends."

She laughed at the joke and hugged him, "How the hell are we going to keep this up?"

"One day at a time. It will be over soon," he told her. The words were for himself as much as her. "Thank you again for coming with me, Valery."

"You owe me." He couldn't tell if she was joking or not. Calvin sighed, "Let's go get intoxicated."

"We're doing this to live. Would being a janitor be that bad?" Valery asked him as Calvin laughed, "We ditched that life for a reason."

"You call this a life? We're just indulging in empty pleasures and killing people. I think we're made to be degenerates to be easily controlled." Valery told him. Calvin sighed, "Probably right. "Guilty pleasures are pleasures nevertheless."

"Not this time." She softly told him composed herself and they both left the fan room with another couple quickly running in. She looked back at him, "You're really disappointed? This is wrong."

"When was the last right thing we did?" Calvin asked her as she gasped pointing at him, "You've really lost it."

The Pandora was still undergoing repairs from the last battle. The refits did wonders to bring the old ship back to life. She still showed signs of her age with cracks in the hull. Calvin and Valery did their best to stay out of the way as the crew performed their jobs making repairs. As they passed by medical, people were being dragged in either on stretchers or in body bags. There were carts filled with left armor taken off the dead or wounded still stained with blood and guts. Sections of the passageways were being fixed up with patchwork. Valery sighed, "How long are we going to be able to keep this up?"

"Long enough. Too late to have reservations now. Just a fact." He tried softening the situation the best he could. On their way back to berthing they happened by the mess deck. It was filled with wounded being treated. On one side were the living, and on the other were the dead. One by one they were stripped and thrown into bags. "You all can take a lot of abuse."

They looked down seeing, Sophia standing next to them. Valery gasped, "Fuck, you're sneaky!"

"I am trying to kill myself and replace her. It kind of helps to be sly," she told them, surprised by the amount of blood and gore. "Wish there was an easier way."

"Don't we all. What ever happened to that prisoner we captured?" Calvin asked her as Sophia sighed, "Lured her into a false sense of security, got what I wanted and killed her."

"Huh?" Valery was surprised by her brutality. "Who am I to judge?"

"I know what you two freaks have been up to. Believe you all have another saying. Can't make an omelet without breaking some eggs?" she mentioned as another crewmember was placed into a body bag and zipped up.

"We're the only timeline that fit your parameters?" Calvin asked her. Sophia nodded, "Universe might be infinite, but limited options on where one can go in a pinch."

"Who ordered the attack on our system?" Valery asked her bluntly. Sophia looked up, "My counterpart, the one I'm trying to replace. Need more motivation to succeed?"

"This is convenient." Valery scoffed.

113

"You know the planet we're heading to is going to be a blood bath, right?" Calvin asked her bluntly, knowing the whole fleet wanted vengeance for Sol.

"Acceptable casualties," Sophia coldly responded. Valery asked, "What other favor would be so great you'd not kill us to cover your tracks?"

"If there's another nation I want dealt with, I can use you all to do it for me. Why waste resources when a friend can do it for me?" She told them with a smile. Calvin found an odd security in that favor as it would mean the survival of the home system. "Sounds reasonable."

"As reasonable as can be in this cutthroat space time we live. For what it's worth though, I don't condone the actions of my counterpart and hope you make her die badly," Sophia told him. "I'm going to take a nap. Talk to you all again eventually."

Valery sighed, "That little runt is scary."

"Yeah. Let's get some rest while we can," Calvin told her as they both went to their berthing. They both walked in as quietly as they could, not wanting to wake anyone else up. They found Hail sleeping on the couch with Barbra next to him. They were watching a light show.

"Huh... this is strange," Calvin commented quietly. Barbra sighed, "We're on a sinking boat with no life rafts. Why not?"

"Good point," Valery told her as they took a seat next to them. "How are you two holding up?"

"Better than Lydia and Audie. They're on a bender in one of the fan rooms," she told them. Calvin nodded, "Sounds depressing and fun."

"Hail and I are pissed that we got the short sticks. No one is going to notice that we're gone with... others just like us back home," Barbra pointed out. Calving tried encouraging her, "They'll know about us and remember. Copies will be the ones envious of us."

"I think they're glad to be absent for once." Valery sighed.

114

"Think his... brother will take that road trip you mentioned? From bottom tip of South America to Alaska," Barbra wondered. Calvin told her, "We'll make sure that happens. Put that camera to good use."

"I heard about that and the recordings. Command used it as motivation. Worked. Yet again I'm envious of Vera and Yeager," she confessed to them. Valery asked, "Really?"

"They got a choice to do what they wanted instead of having it made for them. This Hail and I didn't," she replied with a hint of bitterness in her voice. Calvin nodded. "We both know that pain of no agency."

Barbra laughed, "You two had a Deus Ex Machina save you. Not going to happen twice."

"We're not that lucky. Don't need it because we're talented," Valery told her making her laugh. "Right."

"Ye of little faith," Calvin scoffed jokingly. Barbra nodded at him. The four of them sat around seeing the holographic show change as it went on. Barbra let out a sigh, "Is it sad that these last few months are the best of my life so far?"

"Not really. Means you're burning bright with what little time you have." Calvin told her. Hail laughed, "Better to burn out than to fade away. Right, old man?"

"Don't remember saying that, but good saying as any," Calvin told him trying to calm his own nerves as well as everyone else's. Mission was already going wrong, and the Valkyries know they're coming. Hail sighed, "Do I know you, old man?"

"I would hope so. I'd like to know you better. Seem to be a go getter," Calvin told him wanting to connect with his son. Hail sighed, "Relax. I'm not Yeager. Don't have issues. You raised me as good as a simulation of yourself could."

"Just not the same," Calvin grumbled with regret. Hail laughed, "You didn't have to change my diapers."

"You didn't have chronic diarrhea, did you?"

115

Calvin joked with him as he laughed, "Not my fault. You're the one that fed me crap."

"So ungrateful." The four of them laughed quietly, straining themselves. They went silent again. Hail thought out loud, "Steven had more of a life that I did. Short, but he had his own memories and life. I'm just a copy."

"Set yourself apart then and don't live in the shadow," Calvin told him not wanting to waste time on sorrow, pity or remorse. Barbra nodded, "Good advice."

Calvin rubbed the back of his neck, "Glad you two are adjusting so well. At least I can say I did one thing right."

"Oh, stop being self-loathing." Valery told him as Hail joked, "With all the clones running around, thought you loved yourself."

The four of them cracked up upon hearing him say that. Lydia scoffed, "Degenerates."

Audie asked, "Come back to the rack, honey."

She did and the four were left alone. Barbra laughed, "Curtains are soundproof."

"Ah."

"Are you okay, Senior Chief? Still wondering why you would choose this," she asked him. He was half honest, "I couldn't let my best friend go alone."

"Aw. Aren't you sweet?" Valery saw right through him.

"Friends don't let friends do crazy shit by themselves," he told her as they quieted down and just enjoyed the light show. Each one of them fell asleep on the couch. Calvin was the last one awake as Helena nodded, "You seem ready."

"Not really. Just enjoying the moment," he told her as he closed his eyes, allowing himself to rest.

CHAPTER 17
PREP TIME
2276
ENROOT VALKYRIE SYSTEM
C.S.W. PANDORA
OFFICERS WARDROOM

CALVIN waited in a green padded chair. He looked around seeing other squad leaders, including copies of Rotten and Lane. They gave him an acknowledging nod. Part of him was dismayed that people were getting copied just to get thrown away when they didn't have a choice. The other was glad he wouldn't be facing the end alone. The ward looked luxurious compared to the mess decks for the enlisted. The bulkheads were all holographic. It was currently showing a forest with the wind blowing in the background. It made the room feel larger than it was. If it weren't for people bumping into the bulkhead, he'd think he was back on Earth. Valery sighed, "Boy, doesn't this look fancy."

"Little repair goes a long way," he told her as the doors opened. Someone shouted, "Stand by!"

Everyone stood up at attention. Holly's replicate walked in, "At ease."

Everyone relaxed, sitting back down. Holly started with, "Well if you are feeling suicidal, you've come to the right place. I sent myself on a kamikaze. Let's take down as many of those fuck wits as we can, shall we?"

"Fuck yeah!" Everyone nodded in agreement. Holly nodded, "Okay. Let's get started."

The holographic images changed to a map of the Valkyrie territory. Holly got started, "Our original plan is out the window because all our Trojan Horse ships were either destroyed, too irreparably damaged, or identified as captured. So, we're going to improvise." She paused zooming in on the galactic map on the territory they were aiming for. "With the bitch slapping we just gave those midgets they're gathering up everything they can to come after us. We'll make them think that we're still gunning for their home system when this is our actual target." A planet was highlighted in a heavy populated frontier area. "The operation had been named 'St. Nazaire' for one of the greatest raids of Earth's Second World War."

Helena was standing behind Calvin, "I thought you were mad."

He grumbled, wanting her to shut up. Everyone in the room looked at each other confused and shocked that this was the action they were taking. Holly went on, "There is method to the madness. Now from what information we've been able to gather from our prisoners, they'll have traps in the system waiting for us. We're springing them. While we spring the traps…" the map expanded showing a Claw fleet nearby, "… our allies will create a ghost fleet to strike them. We're going to give them that opening. The rest of the Claw forces are going to throw everything they have at the Valkyries to keep their eyes and reinforcements away from their new home system long enough for us to do what we need to."

Holly had the magnification zoomed in towards the planets. "This planet is a target rich environment to shoot anything and everything that moves. This is all or nothing, so we're throwing everything we can at their main fortress. We'll follow the old plan in taking their generals and admirals hostage to sue for peace." This part was a lie. Calvin kept his mouth shut about that as the clone went on, "We don't want a long, drawn-out war. Trust me on that one. The Dragon's Teeth isn't going to save us. It will, however, give us just enough where we can deliver one hell of a punch. I cannot emphasize enough that this is a one-way trip. Hold nothing back, give nothing to them and remember to avenge those that have been lost. Whenever you think about showing mercy or compassion, remember the 60 billion people those fucks killed and inflict the same pain on them!"

Helena was inspired and yelled, "Fuck yeah!"

Holly went on, "If you all have any questions, now is the time. After this, we're going in."

Valery asked, "Ma'am, is this a one-way trip?"

"We either win or die. That's the only two ways this will end. Fleet will cover the ground forces for as long as they're operational. Things get bleak, kamikaze. Take them with us," Holly told them. The map vanished, and the room turned white. "If there are no other questions, pass along the information to your teams. Dismissed and good luck."

Everyone stood up and filed out of the room. Lane and Rotten went over to Calvin and Valery. "So, this is it?"

"Yeah, looks like it. Sympathies for getting the short stick," Calvin told them as Lane laughed, "Sympathies for being dumb enough to join us."

"Touché."

"Who knows? Maybe we'll get a second... who am I kidding?" Rotten stopped himself, knowing the facts. Valery sighed, "It was worth a shot."

"Someone must. Never say die after all," Calvin told her while trying not to panic. Rotten nodded, "Glad we drank them while we had them, right?"

"Yeah," they both replied to him. Rotten patted them both on the shoulders and asked, "Shall we spread the good news?"

"Good?" Valery asked him as the three of them walked out. Rotten laughed, "Don't you all get sappy. When this is over, we'll have one hell of an after party!"

"Sure, we will," Calvin said with. Lane brought up,

"We'll save a drink for Hank, Rose, Alan, Beth, Katlin, Zara, Cage and all the copies."

"Don't forget about Damon, Tory and Greg, too." Rotten mentioned with a tear coming out of his eye. Calvin mentioned, "Vera, Alec, Yeager, Jane, Mira, Conner, Kathryn and Steven."

"Don't forget us, too." Valery told them.

"Drinks all around," Calvin joked with them as they all started taking their own ways to meet up with their separate squadrons. Helena stuck next to Calvin, "You're all fucked. You know that, right?"

"Aren't you a ray of sunshine?" he asked her sarcastically. The crew was making last minute preparations for the battle to come, adding extra auto turrets, bringing many more weapons and ammo on board, reinforcing the bulkheads, and getting rid of anything unnecessary. "You do know that resurrection is still flaky at best, especially now that you're getting up there in numbers."

"Shut up!" Calvin snapped at her, losing his temper. Valery sighed, "She's only imaginary. Why's she being a bitch?"

Thankfully, no one else heard him shouting that. She laughed, "Think of it as a test."

"Again, if I die, so do you," he told her. Valery scoffed, "Enough suicide jokes."

Helena nodded, "Be with you every step of the way."

"Isn't that great?" He told her as they entered the classroom. Everyone looked up as he walked in. Calvin smiled at them, "Good news. We're going in first."

"That doesn't sound like good news," Audie told him. Lydia scoffed, "He was being sarcastic."

"I know," he grumbled. Hail and Barbra weren't saying much as they were still trying to wake up. Calvin pulled up holographic images of the Pandora and the rest of the battle group. "This is it. We're the tip of the spear!"

"Does that mean we're getting the shaft?" Lydia asked in dismay. Barbra laughed, "You know it!"

"Let us lube you up then," Valery joked with them as Calvin looked at his holo pad and brought up information, "Nice to see you all have lowered expectations. Well, in case there are any EMP devices, remember that there's an off switch in your Mech. It will automatically reboot after a few seconds. Better to be a sitting duck for a short while than be dead in the water permanently. Our objective is to clear out the orbital defenses around their world. It's going to be heavily defended to say the least. We must clear the way for the Marines to go planet side. Sooner they do, sooner they can do the switch. Knowing our luck, the Pandora will get shot down and we'll have to go planet side, too. This is going to be rough. Think of it this way. We are the ones coming to conquer and not the other way around. Remember what they did to our home system? Let's return the favor to them."

"Fuck yeah!" Everyone shouted with pride. Then Barbra's clone pointed out, "Wait, didn't Holly cause... wait, never mind."

"Not really. She just hopped over here to benefit from the bomb. Also, she's throwing another version of herself under the bus..." Valery paused before she just stopped all together.

Calvin sighed, "Just be ready to go in the Hanger Bay in five hours. Make the most of the time given to make sure that we're good to go. Dismissed." All of them stood up and left except Hail. He walked up to him, "So this is actually happening, isn't it?"

"Yeah, you ready, Son?" he asked him. Hail looked at him with concern, "You're in the double digits now. Is there no way that you could...?"

"No. We're all in the same situation. Out of all my children, you're the one that I'll be with at the end. Others are going to be envious of it," he told him while walking up and giving him a hug. Hail laughed, "You're getting overly sappy, old man."

"Just wanted to get something right this time," he told him as Valery sighed, "Wish I had a camera."

"We'll remember this. That's enough," he told her while they headed toward the exit. "Think you and Barbra would go great together."

"Thanks. You'll be a grandfather in no time," he told him as they both nodded, thinking about a future that will never be. The thought would keep them occupied long enough.

CHAPTER 18
LAUNCH AND JOY
2276
VALKYRIE SYSTEM
C.S.W. PANDORA
FAN ROOM

CALVIN walked into the fan room. Holly was waiting for him, "For a second there I didn't think you'd accept my invitation."

"I need to blow off steam as much as you do. Way to pull rank by the way. So, are you a cheap copy or new and improved over the original?" Both started to take off their armored suits and clothing as quickly as they could while walking up to each other. "Rank does have its privileges. I'm improved, thank you very much."

They both met in the center of the room and started kissing. Their arms wrapped around their bodies while their tongues slid into each other's open mouths. Holly gasped, "So wish we weren't pressed for time!"

"Let's make the most of what we have then." They locked their mouths together again. Calvin used his hands to massage her back, slowly working downwards, feeling the curves in her body. The heat between them started to make them sweat. Holly sighed in between kisses, "To hell with hurry up and wait!"

She reached down, grabbed him and guided him where he needed to go. The heat in the room seemed to go up as they connected with each other. Both leaned into one another, allowing the sensations to kick in. Holly bit down on his shoulder as he went further. Holly's nails scratched his back leaving long scratches on his skin. He kissed her on her neck as he slowly moved back to tease her with the next push. She couldn't wait as she moved forward meeting him. He lifted one of her legs up and pushed back. Her arms felt like they were going to crush his shoulders as he moved himself. He kept supporting her as both got into a rhythm. Calvin got a good look at her chest as it stayed firm while bouncing in the moment. Holly gasped, "Change positions!"

"What?" he said as she moved off and got on her hands and knees. "This could be the last time. I want to do all of them."

He was at a loss for words seeing her in that position. The light seemed to shimmer off her skin. He reached forward, feeling her smooth skin and firm backside. Calvin got up behind her as she lifted herself higher up tantalizing him. He knelt and pushed with everything he had. He grabbed her sides and held on as she pushed back against him. They made a loud slap as they slammed together. He reached around and massaged her sensitive parts while moving. She gasped, leaning back and kissing him before dropping back down with a loud gasp. While keeping his concentration, Calvin kept pressure on her in more ways than one, making her yelp. She then shoved back hard enough to cause him to fall on to his back, and she sat down on top of him. He sat back up and used his legs to push upwards. She came back down with each push. Calvin reached up with one arm around her and started to massage her chest. He used the other to massage more sensitive parts of her. Both of their bodies were drenched in sweat and pooled on the deck below them. She laughed, "Great programming!"

Calvin smiled, not caring about anything other than the moment. Holly spread her legs wider to support their movements. She then lifted herself up, spun around and dropped herself on top of him making him fall back to the deck. Holly leaned down and kissed him. He moved his head up and pushed his lips against hers. Their tongues went around one another's in a crucial motion. Calvin pushed her forward and got on top of her. He used the momentum to push down deeper into her. She reached up and hugged him again as they slid across the deck with each thrust. When they got back to the bulkhead they were standing again. Calvin was supporting her spread legs while she grabbed his shoulder again. He didn't let the loud knock disrupt his concentration. He started to feel a hardening sensation as he neared his climax. She was gripping tighter and tighter. They both moved as fast as they could, and she let out a loud gasp. They both moved against each other as they climaxed and dropped down to the deck on their sides. He gave a couple more thrusts before he was done. Calvin smiled, "I think I'm starting to like you, even if you are cannon fodder."

"We're all cannon fodder here, honey!" She smiled and gave him a kiss as there was a hard knock on the door. Holly sighed, "Really wish we could bask for a minute. Wish a lot of things were different."

"Yeah, others want to have fun, too," he told her. Reluctantly, they both dressed quickly. Once their armored suits were back on, they opened the door to eight people in less advanced armored suits waiting to go in. One asked bitterly, "How come they got to fuck by themselves?"

"Because she's an Admiral, dipshit. That's why," someone explained to her. Holly huffed, "Earned what I got, you bastards!"

"Who cares? We don't have long!" one of them said as they all piled in taking off their suits. The doors closed as another group came up behind them. "Shit!"

"Why not use a berthing?" Calvin asked them. "Because they're fucking packed already!" one of them answered.

"Oh. I'm guessing the other fan room is full, too." Calvin wondered as Holly pulled him away, "Come on.

Need to stand by again."

They got up to the hanger doors. "If we survive this, we should go on leave together."

"Some place tropical. Hawaii when it's restored," he told her as she laughed, "We can dream. Look, watch your back out there. Don't let Helena keep you down."

"What?" Calvin asked concerned by what she said and his eyes going wide. She smiled and grabbed his crotch, "I actually kind of like you. Remember that when the finish line comes up." Holly gave him one last kiss. "I'll see you out there soon enough."

"Yeah," he halfheartedly told her as he went back into the hanger. His Titan was waiting for him. One arm held what looked like a bazooka and the other a cannon that looked like a machine gun. He looked up into the eyes of the humanoid machine as it lay dormant waiting for him to take control. Each Titan had a modified transport at its disposal. It had extra weapons, extra parts, and could act as a shield. Calvin got into his cockpit and onto the comms link with his teammates. Lydia told him, "Still nothing."

"We've been waiting for eleven hours!" Barbra shouted. Audie sighed, "Some things never change. Hurry up and wait still applies."

"How long were the lines to...?" Barbra asked when she got interrupted by Lydia who told, "We can join the next orgy when we get the chance, right, senior?"

"Don't take too long," he told them, feeling a little embarrassed. He also didn't want to start an argument. Valery sighed, "How was the copy?"

"More tender than the original. Who were you with?" he wondered as she sighed, "Strangers. Also, I don't want my last memory of you to be another disgraceful masturbation session."

"I understand," he told her slightly disappointed. Yet knew it was for the best. Helena then shouted, "You are a true psycho pervert. Try sleeping with yourself again after hooking up with a copy of a woman that will be the end of you."

"She might be a figment of your imagination Calvin, but she has a point." Valery sighed, getting annoyed with their looming insanity.

Barbra asked him, "Uh, shouldn't we be more professional? Also, why is the command allowing everyone to fornicate like rabbits?" Calvin sighed, "Go have some fun. Our time is short. Want to go for the faulty beacon or the museum with booze?"

Hail sighed, "I understood that reference. Drink up."

"Well, the chain of command probably doesn't give a shit if they get caught. They can't punish the dead," Audie guessed. Barbra then asked, "How come even though we're technically machines, we carried over a shit load of trades from our organic ancestors?"

"Made in their image or what they wanted to be?" Hail guessed. Calvin replied, "Tall sexy orgasmic tornadoes of destruction?"

"No. Because degenerates are easy to control," Valery chimed in.

"That's one way to put it," Barbra replied, feeling the existentialism and mortality weighing down on her. Hail joked, "Am I going have a stepmother soon?"

"If we somehow don't die, maybe," Calvin pointed out.

Valery spoke up, "Okay, we just got an update."

Calvin showed the others the information that revealed the system was packed full of ships, weapons platforms, mines, and jammers. Lydia sighed, "So glad we're not the decoys for once!"

"You know we are!" Audie scoffed.

Calvin told them, "New set of objectives just popped up. We need to take out the jammers and mines around the slip gate. The jammers can cause us to die permanently. There is a contingency that if we get killed, we'll be brought back with a few memories forgotten. This also brings on the potential risk of mental insanity. So, let's try not to get killed until the end."

"Don't need to tell us twice. One hell of a time to be changing plans!" Valery sighed.

"I forgot to ask. How come we aren't using the whole fleet in this operation? I mean draining the Claws resources is one thing, but this just seems petty!" Lydia asked. Hail explained, "We're the ones springing traps, too. Don't want to go all in if we don't know what we're getting into. Anything could be waiting for us in the system."

A voice boomed over the intercom, "Attention Consortium forces, Admiral Holly Murphy speaking."

"She took your last name?" Calvin asked his imaginary friend Helena while she smiled, "I gave it to her."

"Shut up imaginary friend!" Valery snapped.

Everyone went quiet. There was nothing but the soft abeyant sounds around them as they waited to hear what she was going to say. Holly came on, "Greetings. You know who I am. You know what I've done. Now what you should question is what you'll be doing in the next hour. As you may or may not have heard, I and others have gotten a message from the Valkyrie forces. They want us to surrender. Those condescending bastards said they weren't going to negotiate with a pack of nonfunctioning machines following orders from a dead race. Let that sink in along with all the other horrible things they've caused. They not only created a living hell for our people back in the home system for decades; they caused the zombies to exist. They caused the death and suffering of billions, possibly even trillions. They tried to kill us repeatedly while calling us a potential threat. They said that all the terrible things were just favors for us. Let's return a favor to these arrogant pricks with prejudice. They only mercy those bastards are getting is our genitals. When we're done, all will see our work and get the hint; fucking with us is a bad idea! You all know what to do. Kill them all!"

"Kill them all!" started to get chanted over the comm. It got louder and louder with each passing second. It was amplified by the sound of chest pounding, too. There was a sudden high-pitched screech that silenced everyone. Holly finished with, "We have a job to do. I'll be leading from the front. Follow me in with weapons free and ready to fire."

Calvin accessed a camera feed seeing the Pandora and the rest of the battle group form up behind the heavier cruisers and dreadnoughts. They took the lead as it and several hundred other vessels started moving next to them in mass formations. The Valkyrie fleet held its position. In an instant, both groups fired at one another. The beams of light were only visible on a certain spectrum. When a ship's energy shield would pop, the whole vessel would soon get torn apart by weapons fire. When the dreadnoughts opened fire, they took out multiple ships in one salvo. They kept up a constant rate of fire, but the ships were holding their own against almost the whole enemy fleet. No matter what they threw at them, the mighty dreadnoughts' shields seemed to either absorb or deflect the rounds. All the defense platforms targeted the massive ships. The destroyers, frigates and cruisers engaged one another. The Hawk Fighters and target Condor Transports flew out from their ships like bees leaving the nest along with the Titans. They were soon engaging the groups of Harpies and Emerald fighters. There were several small flashes of light for every machine that was destroyed. The jammers were illuminated by the HUDs showing what they needed to target. They looked like asteroids with antennas sticking out of them. "The Pandora is going to use its weaponry to take them out from afar. Our job is going to be to find mines before they hit any of the capital ships. Keep on the lookout for Harpies, too," command said over the comms.

"Roger," everyone replied. Calvin felt anticipation

as his Titan climbed on top of the modified Condor as it moved into launch position. The doors in front of him opened and he saw the lights start at red and then flash yellow. Holly told them all, "Give them hell!"

"Fuck yeah!" they all shouted as the lights turn green. Calvin felt a rush as he was launched out of the ship along with the others. They were facing the massive slip gates. It still looked almost as good as new. Once all the craft were clear, the Pandora and other ships in the front opened fire, taking out several of the jammers. It didn't take too many rounds before they went up in an explosion. The Hawks and Condors moved up a bit, yet not far enough to get into the line of fire of the capital ships. There were only seventy ships in their battle group. All of them were fast moving destroyers and cruisers. One of the nearby transports ran into a mine and caused a massive explosion that took out the whole wing of the small craft. Calvin shouted at them, "Don't just blindly rush ahead!"

"We're not the ones that did!" Valery shouted as she fired at a mine. It exploded in a bright flash. Several other mines were illuminated for a brief second, and the others opened fire taking them out. It took multiple rounds to get them to go off. The ships behind them got closer and closer as the fighters slowed down, unable to destroy them all quickly enough. Holly yelled, "Okay, change in plans! We'll light them up for the heavies to take out, Roger?"

"Got it," the others replied as they fired just enough rounds to expose the mine before the large ships took them out with a laser blast. The debris bounced off their shielding as they pushed ahead. The Gate seemed to grow as they got closer and closer to it. Then in front of them several ships suddenly became visible for a brief second. They all fired on one Consortium ship at the same time. The destroyer was ripped apart by the weapons fire and exploded from the inside out. Before any of the other ships could react, they vanished. Hail grumbled, "Guess they upgraded their stealth drives."

"No fucking shit! Let's find those assholes before they take another shot!" Calvin told them. All the Titans went ahead and started firing in random directions. Barbra managed to score a hit. The others fired on the target, giving its location away for the other ships to shoot her down. The hits exposed the ship completely before the hull was ripped open. Two torpedoes made each half rip apart. Again, the stealth ships appeared and opened fire. This time the Consortium vessels were quick on the trigger and got three of them before they vanished again. Yet another destroyer was shredded by the weapons fire. Then another ship ran into multiple mines. They seemed to come out of nowhere and crash into the ship. The blast was strong enough to take out the whole vessel. All the ships started firing randomly ahead of themselves as the small craft fell back. Several mines went off in front of them. A couple of Valkyrie ships were also illuminated. Once they were, the ships got blown apart with torpedoes ripping into them. Audie shouted, "Harpies incoming!"

Calvin checked his HUD, and it pointed where they were coming from. They were being followed by multiple mines. Without thinking, they all went ahead to stop them. Calvin noticed they were in range of the jammers. He kept his distance as he fired proximity missiles at his target. The Harpies managed to shoot several of them down, but not enough. One got in behind and exploded, taking out all the mines and the machine. There were several flashes of light as the explosives went off ahead of them. Suddenly, one of the cruisers got hit by mines, a laser blast, and torpedoes all at once. She went out in a bang. All the ships kept their speed as they pressed on despite the losses. Barbra asked, "Didn't we have stealth tech, too? Why the hell aren't we using it? Should we have an easier time detecting them?"

"We're probably playing decoy again!" Audie shouted at her. Lydia then shot up, "That fucking figures!"

"Quit your bitching and kill these fuckers!" Valery shouted at them, scoring a hit on a Harpy.

Calvin grumbled and shouted back, "Let's give those pricks something to pay attention to then!"

Another set of mines went off just ahead almost blinding them. Suddenly, the bright light was replaced with several Valkyrie ships. The whole squadron bounced off the ship's shields. A couple other Titans exploded on impact, hitting the ship too hard. As Calvin spun out of control, three hundred ships appeared, surrounding them. "Shit!"

The Consortium ships came together, banding their shields to one another as the mines started to fly at them. Calvin shouted, "Get back in the Pandora now!"

All the fighters, transports, and Titans scrambled to get back inside their motherships. Each of them came crashing back inside the hanger bay. When the last craft was inside, the entry battle group went to warp and got outside the net of the Valkyrie vessels. The Valkyrie fleet scrambled to adjust its position as the Consortium ships all fired at once. They managed to take out fifty ships before the enemy was able to regroup. Despite the losses, the Valkyries still outnumbered them. They fired back taking out twelve more ships. Calvin shouted, "Back out!"

All the small craft were thrown back out into the fray as torpedoes flew past them. A single Valkyrie ship was illuminated in their HUDs. "We're doing modified kamikazes. At the last second, ditch your Condors and fly off in your Titans. Got it?"

"Roger," They all replied as they sped forward toward the massive ship as the Harpies flew at them. Calvin's Condor took multiple hits from them. The shields went out and the outer armor began to fly off with every hit. The others weren't having much luck either. The Pandora fired several laser rounds to get them to back off. The dreadnought they were heading toward fired a torpedo burst at them. Calvin had to ditch his transport early, as it was taken out by one of the explosives. He quickly engaged several Harpies by himself. He covered the others as they kept up their suicidal course. Calvin used his dual-wheeled rocket launchers to fire several proximity missiles at the Harpies. He quickly emptied the mag as the enemy machines were forced back. Two of them were cut in half from the rounds exploding next to them. Calvin quickly reloaded and fired again. He shot off in any direction where there weren't friendlies, always scoring a hit with the pull of his triggers. Suddenly, both of his launchers were shot from his hands. He moved back as they were blown apart. He pulled out two massive hand-held cannons and kept firing. His Mech mechanical hand yanked back on the triggers, firing off more proximity rounds. He moved backwards, dodging the rounds that came at him. A warning flashed before his eyes, and he quickly rolled out of the way of a laser blast that came from behind him. His two cannons melted along with parts of his external armor. He ditched the damaged weapons and his extra armored plates. The rest of his squadron managed to get close enough to where each one was able to send their transports flying into the massive vessel. All the Titans quickly flew off, flying away from the massive ship as the transports crashed into the vessel, one right after the other. They all exploded at the same time creating a massive rupture in the ship's hull. Several of the Consortium ships fired at the breach, splitting the ship in two. Both halves got a torpedo shot into its ruptured sections, making both of them burst apart. The Titans moved back to the Pandora as the Harpies chased after them. As they pulled back, Lydia took several hits. Her limbs were blown off and she started spiraling out of control. As her damaged Titan went off to the side she asked, "Am I in the clear?"

"Yeah..." Calvin told her. She laughed after getting hit again, "Why didn't I believe..."

Her Titan blew up from the damage it had taken. Audie shouted bitterly, "Motherfuckers!" Audie shouted again as he quickly took out a Harpy with one of his cannons. One of his arms got shot off along with his extra armor. Hail went up to him and pulled him back, "Don't be a hero!"

He fired off several decoys from his torso giving them an escape; he replied, "Wasn't planning on it."

Valery and Barbra covered them as they got closer to the Pandora. Several Consortium ships around them were struck with torpedoes and were taken out. All of them had to move to dodge the fragments of the destroyed vessels. One of the fragments hit Barbra's Titan, taking both her legs out. Calvin rushed over to her and pulled her back to the Cruiser. They hid behind the Pandora as her shields protected them. As another destroyer next to them was torn apart by laser fire, it became apparent they were surrounded again. This time all the ships had taken multiple hits and weren't going to be able to run. Helena started to laugh. Calvin wondered, "What so fucking funny? We're all about to die?"

"Not us. Them." She said as the slip gate suddenly became active. Thousands of Claw ships flew through the gate. The Valkyrie ships didn't stand a chance as they were quickly shot to shreds. Some of them were blown up by the mines, but it was a drop in the bucket as the reinforcements kept flying in. Valery shouted, "This better be the last fucking time we're fucking decoys!"

"You know it won't be. Just be thankful we're not dead. Everyone back on the Pandora for repairs." Calvin told them as they all flew back to the ship.

CHAPTER 19
DISTRESS
2276
VALKYRIE SYSTEM
C.S.W. PANDORA
HANGER BAY

ALL their Titans landed. Barbra needed help, having no legs to land on. Quickly the crewmembers were hard at work repairing each of their suits, replacing limbs, weapons, and armor. All the Titans once fixed were placed on top of new modified transports. Audie quickly asked, "Is Lydia alive?"

"I'm fine!" She told them as she walked back into the hanger. It didn't take long before they were all good to go again. Ground crews were amazingly proficient at making repairs. They all waited inside their Titans for what felt like the longest time, cooling off from the first round of fighting. Calvin tapped back into the camera feeds and saw outside. The combined Claw and Consortium forces were making progress pushing the Valkyrie fleet back. It was amazing seeing so many ships battling it out. The stream of reinforcements seemed nonstop. All the Valkyrie ships seemed to be pulling back to the inhabited worlds. He adjusted his line of vision and saw that there were massive shields around each planet. "I think they're up to something!"

"You and everyone else in the fleet. Everyone

seems to be pulling back," Hail told him as every ship started moving away from the Valkyrie positions. Calvin shouted, "EMP! Turn everything off!"

Everyone did so as quickly as they could. Everything in the ship went dark and Calvin was stuck inside his Mech with the machine turned off. He sat in the dark waiting for something to happen. Helena told him, "Everything is going to be okay."

"You are borderline bipolar," he told his imaginary friend. She laughed, "What? Everyone plays with your emotions. Why not me?"

"One too many," Calvin told her as the ship rocked. Thankfully, soon the light flashed back on, and he was suddenly seeing the lights of his cockpit again. His Titan was reactivated, and he saw out of the camera feed again. He saw the backup force showed up just in time to prevent the main fleet from being wiped out. They were holding the line as all the ships got back up and running. Then he saw something that caught his attention: Marine transports that were making their drops planet side. The giant amphibious ships were taking a pounding as they went in for their assault. They were coming into the atmosphere like meteors. As the ships came back, they all scrambled to join the drop ships to give them cover as they made their landing. The Claws took the brunt of the assault, with their numbers cut in half. What ships they had left formed a perimeter around the slip gate to buy themselves time for more forces to gather up. The stream of reinforcements, on the other hand, started to thin out. Fewer ships were coming through. It also looked like several Consortium vessels discreetly fled as well. "What the hell?" Calvin saw a set of orders pop up in front of him and he let out a sigh, "Hate to tell you all this, but we're joining the assault forces."

"Who didn't see this coming?" Valery asked them, accepting her fate.

"Shit," Audie grumbled knowing what was in store

for them. Hail sighed, "Well, didn't take long for us to get re-tasked."

"I didn't want to live forever anyway," Calvin told them jokingly. The Pandora and all the other ships that were left in the battle group headed in towards the fortress world. Most of the Valkyrie fleet was focused on the Claws, giving them time to move. Helena asked him, "Do you dream?"

"Do you shut up?" he asked her, focusing on launching again. The lights started flashing as their Titans hopped back on top of the transports. Hail said, "Let's hope most of the jammers have been taken out."

"Don't need them. Don't plan on dying," Barbra boldly said. Valery told her, "Don't make plans unless you're willing to break them."

"We're all on borrowed time. Make it count for something. Be offensive to the end!" Calvin said looking at the lights. He saw the lights go green again. He and the others were thrown back out into the fray. They focused fire on the orbital platforms that were harassing the dropships. The green and blue planet below looked like Earth. It got cloudy with the hundreds of ships descending onto the world. The dropships went full speed ahead as they started their descent down to the planet. Several practical rounds flew past them from the planet and the ships in front of them. Barbra shouted, "This is fucking extreme just to get even!"

"Just roll with it!" Valery shouted at her as a Valkyrie firing platform in front of them got shot to pieces. They all opened fire on the Harpies as they tried to escape. Their burnt parts flew past them after being destroyed. Calvin ordered, "Stay behind the Pandora! Let the heavies do the bashing while we follow in behind them!"

All the small craft pulled behind the large ship as they got closer to the planet. They could start making out cities down below. They saw clouds moving and mixing in with the smoke clouds from the bombardment. Several

Valkyrie ships still fought on to hold off the wave of vessels coming at them. The larger ships broke off and stayed outside the planet's atmosphere. They'd hold the line while the smaller ships charged in, descending onto the planet. The Cruisers and Dreadnoughts provided cover fire. The swarm of vessels would move out of the way of the rounds as they flew past them. Pandora led the charge of the smaller ships taking heavy fire. It rocked with every hit the shields took. The Valkyries weren't going out quietly. Some of the ships did kamikazes on the incoming vessels. One of the dropships got destroyed when one of the crystal ships slammed into it. They both went up exploding and taking out a cluster of small craft nearby them. The fleet quickly adapted and moved out of the way of the suicidal ships and let the capital ships behind them shoot them to bits. Soon things became crowded with so many vessels and transports all trying to get planet side. The Valkyries took advantage of this and fired spreads of torpedoes at the ships. One Claw destroyer ahead of them was ripped apart by the salvo. Two more destroyers were hit and crashed into each other. Both seemed to disintegrate as they pushed into one another. The Pandora blocked the debris as they flew right through it. Soon several ships broke off to allow others to maneuver. A frigate was torn apart by a swarm of torpedoes as it acted as a shield for the rest of the group. It fell apart as it dropped into the atmosphere. The Valkyrie formations gave way to the onslaught, with multiple ships flying right past them. The orbiting capital vessels picked them off as they were getting cut apart from almost every direction. They clustered together in their last stand against the horde. Group by group they were taken out in a fury of torpedoes and plasma rounds. They were showered in energized projectiles that battered the vessels. In seconds, their hulls were ripped open, laser blast cut deeper into the dying hulks. Their hulls sent a shower of shimmering dust into space as they bent and ruptured. Some of them had escape pods launching from them. The pods were picked up by the transports and taken back to their motherships as trophies. Almost all the Harpies were either destroyed or went to the surface. Calvin shouted, "We're going planet side to assure the Marines are able to get a beach head! Brace for entry! It's going to be rough!"

"It's the way the Valks like it!" Valery shouted as the front of the Pandora started glowing red as they entered the atmosphere. This left them vulnerable to attacks. A salvo of torpedoes flew up at the ships and multiple vessels were destroyed. The orbiting ships fired as many torpedoes as they could throw out to cover the descending ships. All of them coming down at once looked like a widespread thunderstorm. Soon everything stopped shaking and things went from black to blue. Calvin heard the sound again and felt the shockwaves through the air. There were flashes of red and orange that lasted much longer than just a few seconds. Calvin told them, "Time to run the gauntlet! Same thing we did the last time. Send out our Condors on a kamikaze with the planetary guns. After that, we're pounding ground with the rest of the grunts!"

"Going to drive those fuckers into submission," Lydia shouted. Audie laughed, "Hell yeah!"

"Easier said than done. Hate to point this out, but there's a fuck ton of jammers all over the place. And take a better look below," Barbra pointed out. They were dropping down on the outskirts of a wooden area that was right next to a metropolis that looked like a hive of glass. All the buildings were angled like diamonds and shimmered in the light. As the ground became clearer, they came under heavy fire from below. From behind them, torpedoes came crashing down into the surface causing a massive crater to form in the ground. It sent a huge geyser of dirt into the air followed by a flash of red and orange. All the Harpies were falling back into the city that was protected by an energy shield. It flashed repeatedly with each strike it took. The planetary weapons fired up in the air. Some were taken out by torpedoes and others managed to escape with their shields still up. As the transports came down, they all came under fire from the city as well as the ground forces in front of them. Several transports were knocked out of the sky and sent crashing into the dirt. Calvin set his Condor to fly into the cannon and pushed the transport's engines to the max. He ejected his Titan from the machine and the Condor crashed into the cannon. It went up in a flash as the tube went flat on the deck and all the ordnance went up in flames, leaving a deep crater in the ground. He quickly landed as did the others. They all had to deal with falling debris flying at them from every direction. Some Mechs were shot to pieces before they could even land. Others were dead when they hit the dirt. The only cover they had was the craters made by the bombardment. Calvin fired all the rocket ammo he had at the city. All the rounds exploded when they hit the shield. He ducked down as rounds flew above his head. Hail was lying next to him, "Happy landings, old man?"

"I'd say so seeing as we're not dead!" He replied to him jokingly as more Titans landed in front of them, getting chewed up by weapons fire. The Marines' green colored Titans were not as well armored or equipped at theirs. They only had the most basic of items on them: handheld cannon or rocket launcher and weapons mounted in the round head. The ones that survived the drop huddled around each other linking their shields together. "Why do they call it a beach head anyway?"

"Really thinking about BJs right now?" Lydia shouted as she ducked down next to them. Hail laughed, "You're the one that said it. Not us!"

A Titan's arm flopped down next to him with sparks still flying out of it. Audie and another Titan ran over to them. The second Titan got shot in the torso and the head. Valery made it and shouted, "Shouldn't the damned bombardment have done more?"

"When does a bombardment ever work right?"

Hail asked her. Lydia snapped, "We mastered intergalactic space travel! We should be fucking better with ordnance dropping!"

"You'd think," Barbra shouted at her while the others joined them. Lane laughed, "Glad we could join the party!"

"Where would you be without us?" Rotten asked them as they ducked once more. All around them Mech were hiding in their craters as the rounds kept hitting nearby. Any of them that dared stick their limbs or head out got them shot off. Hail asked, "Any ideas on how to move forward?"

"I've called in for smoke rounds to be dropped! Once they hit, head for the shield. Try to match frequencies when you contact the barrier! Got it," Rotten told them. Calvin nodded, "Got it. What happened to…?"

"They're still on patrol." Lane told him, alluding to their squadrons that were gone.

The rounds soon impacted in front of them and sent smoke into the air. It was thick enough to where they couldn't see anything in front of them. It even affected multiple spectrums of vision. All the Mechs rose out of their craters and charged forward as fast as they could. All the Titans charged together into the fog in front of them blindly. It didn't take long before they reached the shield. Calvin went at it like he was trying to break through a glass wall. He went shoulder first and went past it with a flash. All the smoke was gone, and he was exposed. He suddenly took several hits. His shields went out and parts of his extra armor were blown off. He ditched the rest of it to be lighter and went up against one of the buildings nearby. Calvin suddenly saw several mines placed inside the building. He rocketed up as they went off. The shockwave sent glass showering down on top of the Mechs. The building dropped on top of his squadron. He went down back to the ground and rolled out of the way of the structure. It crumbled as it hit the shield, sending more debris flying.

He adjusted his vision and fired back at the Harpies hiding behind the buildings. Calvin fired his handheld cannon with the round flying through a building and hitting a Harpy in the back, splitting it in half. He quickly had to boost to the side as rounds came flying back at him. Next to him several Mechs fell as they tried to get up to the roofs of the buildings. Rotten shouted, "Grenades!"

He tackled Calvin as they came raining down on top of them. He felt like he was in a drum set that was being played. He fired his cannon up at the roofs, blowing them up. The others that survived the blast followed suit and did the same. Several of the nearby skyscrapers' tops were blown apart. The Harpies boosted off and came under fire from the others. Several were knocked out of the sky by weapons fire. Calvin sighed, "I owe you one."

"Shame you won't be able to pay me back," Rotten told him. "Oh, come on, I'm not one way!"

"Not your fault for once," he told him. Calvin saw his Titan was covered in shrapnel. One went through the machines back and into the cockpit. "Oh shit."

"Ever heard the term angel of death," Rotten asked as his voice got weaker. "You're going to get resurrected! Don't sweat it!"

"Don't be a wuss!" Lane shouted at him. She tried to get to him but was pinned down.

"We're doomed the moment we're copied. Guess we just get everyone killed. Just like a hero… living the dream," Rotten asked him before shouting. "Look out, dipshit!"

Calvin saw a Harpy flying down at him. He boosted out of the way letting Rotten's machine to take the hit. Calvin lunged forward and stuck his cannon's barrel into the Harpy and fired. It ripped in half and flew backwards. He came under fire again, ducked down and fired his cannon. Calvin managed to shoot down two more of them as the others pulled back. All the Mechs simply started to level all the buildings in front of them. It caused a domino effect that had most of the buildings in the city toppling over. The path seemed cleared for them to get to the massive shield generator. It looked like a set of diamonds in the shape of a flower with a fountain of light coming from the center. All the Mechs around them had their back mounted cannons fire at long distance to hit the generator. Calvin followed suit, firing his handheld cannon. Everyone fired their heavy weapons at the generator. There was a massive flash as the shield went down. The sky was clearer than it was before. The destroyers and frigates above started firing at the ground troops as they scattered. The Valkyries pulled back to the mountain where their capital was located. All the Mech mercilessly fired at the Harpies as they tried to get away. Despite the onslaught, several did get away. Audie laughed, "I love destroying things!"

"Yeah…" Calvin said bewildered by what Rotten told him. He saw that they were just out of the range of the jammers. Hail shouted, "Shouldn't we be focused on clearing out more of the orbital guns?"

"No. We go for the prize!" Calvin shouted as more rounds landed near them. As they went off, he saw a round heading towards Barbra, "Head to the mountain!"

He shoved her Titan out of the way and used his shield to block the round. The Titan's right arm got blown off and his machine was sent tumbling backwards. When he regained coherency, he saw five Harpies closing in on him. He quickly fired back with every weapon his machine had while taking multiple hits in the process. One enemy Mech managed to dodge the volley and lunged right at him. He pulled a saber out and both machines stabbed each other at the same time. The two giants slammed onto the ground with the reactor of the Harpy about to go off. Calvin sighed, "Eye on the prize. Eye…"

CHAPTER 20
DOOMED AND HOPEFUL
2276
VALKYRIE SYSTEM
C.S.W. PANDORA
RESURRECTION BAY

ALVIN came up from the pool screaming. He saw the red lights flashing as the ship rocked repeatedly. There weren't any guards there to greet him. The red lights were flickering in the dark. Everything looked wrecked. The liquid in the pool started rising into the air. As he started drifting up, he saw that the number on his arm was now 13A. He gasped, "What the fuck?"

"They say that's an unlucky number. Yet again tell that to eleven and twelve," Helena told him as the ship seemed to go into free fall with alarms going off. A voice shouted, "All hands! Abandon ship! Repeat! Abandon…"

The intercom went down, and the lights went out completely. The liquid rose in the air as the ship plummeted. Helena then shouted at him, "Kick off now!"

He did so, sending his feet into the black void and hitting the bulkhead. He sent himself flying forward and bumped into an armored suit. Not being picky, he quickly put it on. Calvin regained his bearing as his vision came back. He was shocked when he saw his own dead body in front of him with a twelve on his arm. "Shit!"

"If you don't want to end up like him, get to the hanger!" Helena shouted at him. Calvin bashed his way through the debris and flew down the passageways. There were dead crewmen, hanging wires, leaking pipes, free floating metal, and sparks flying. Helena shouted at him, "Take a right. Trust me on this one!"

He didn't argue as he followed her directions. He avoided touching the bulkheads, overheads, and decks as they were starting to crack. The sound of metal being bent and snapping was deafening. Helena shouted at him, "Boost!"

Calvin instinctively used his thrusters to fly forward. A breach ripped through the hull as the ship ripped in half. Calvin could see outside as the vessel tumbled down towards the planet. He got glimpses of the Consortium fleet above being chewed up by the Valkyries, being picked off one by one. They were clustering together in one last desperate attempted to stave off their inevitable destruction. The Claw armada was getting routed back to the slip gate. Most of their ships were retreating. Helena snapped him out of his gazing by shouting, "Move!"

He let himself drop down into the disintegrating vessel, "Left!"

Calvin boosted to his side and started running along the bulkhead. He tried to stay light on his feet as it felt like the surface would give way. Helena shouted at him, "Stop!"

He did, and a spark set off an oxygen tank. Calvin ducked down, avoiding the debris and flames. His shields kept him from being roosted. "Keep going!"

He pushed ahead and saw the hanger bay was coming up. He rocked forward at full speed as the passageway started to collapse in front of him. Inside the hanger, the vehicles that were strapped down were flying out the open doors. The sound of wind roaring drowned out the ship falling apart. Again, he saw the fleet on its last ropes. Several other ships suffered the same fate as they fell apart during free fall. The blue sky seemed to be filled with the debris of the slain vessels. One had their reactor go critical and rip open from the inside with a violent blast.

The shockwave made the hanger bay split in two. Calvin found himself free falling in midair. Helena shouted, "Look out!"

He quickly dodged a fragment that zoomed right by him. Helena appeared next to him and pointed at a Titan that was intact. He quickly used everything he had to fly toward the machine. As it fell back towards the ground, the arms waving in the air seemed to beckon him to the Mech. He saw another destroyer flying towards it as it trailed black smoke. Calvin turned around and flew backward and landed in the cockpit. He quickly interfaced with the machine and got it online. A proximity alarm went off as the ship came at them. He rocked backwards narrowly avoiding the vessel. Once it flew under him, it was struck by a torpedo. It split apart into three different pieces, all falling to the planet below. Pandora went down in flames and fire. Calvin gave her a quick salute. "You got one last fight after all."

He checked his sensors, seeing things were going badly, "What the fuck happened? We're winning! Right?"

"Valkyries managed to shut down the gate and got reinforcements. We got 'Bay of Pigs' today," Helena told him. Calvin knew the reference and snapped back, "Fuck that! Where's the team?"

"Somewhere below you. Got to land safely somehow," she told him as the city below them started to get bigger. There were still signs of fighting going on all around them with explosions popping off all over the place. He saw a Condor that was still flying below him. He started heading towards it as multiple shrapnel rounds burst from above. Calvin had his Titan duck behind a large fragment that was soon penetrated with hot plasma. He boosted back as it seemed to head towards him. Another alarm went off as another debris flew at him. He rocked out of the way as the two hunks of metal slammed into each other. Helena shouted at him, "Use your boosters sparingly and you should have a soft landing. Oh look, there's your team."

He saw a group of Titans fighting it out in the streets as a large group of enemy Mechs were closing in on them. Calvin looked at a building that was about to topple over. Helena laughed, "I think I know where this is going."

Calvin moved his Titan towards the building and slammed into it with full force while using his energy shields to soften the blow. The impact caused the whole structure to pass its tipping point and start to fall. The Harpies all aimed their weapons up at him and tried to shoot him down. He moved to the side letting the building take the hits as they broke rank and tried to flee. Calvin shouted, "Timber, fuckers!"

The building crushed a whole platoon of the machines under its weight in a violent crash. Calvin jetted away from the building and landed next to his teammates. The Titans were held up in a crater barely holding the enemy at bay. Hail sighed, "Nice entrance and all, old man, but you have a trick to stop that?"

"What?" He asked as another building came tumbling on top of them this time. Calvin nodded, "Shields up."

Chapter 21
To the Gate
2276
Valkyrie System
Planet Code Name Valhalla
Outer Edge of Valkyrie
Headquarters

T HE team bashed their way out from the debris of the destroyed building and rushed ahead with their mechanical legs moving them as fast as they could while rounds landed around them. The giant machines were surprisingly nimble moving about the wasteland filled with destroyed ships, structures and debris. They dodged the rounds as they came up. Other Titan units joined them as they made a mad dash toward the mountain. Lane shouted, "Up!"

Everyone stopped as a Condor crashed in front of them. All of them ducked down as the fragments flew over their heads. A Titan behind them was impaled with parts of the debris and fell backwards. Valery sighed, "Dibs on the ammo."

"They just fucking died!" Barbra shouted. Hail told her, "As cold as it sounds, the dead don't need ammo. We do."

Lydia told her, "Don't be selfish. Share!"

"I was going to! Pull my hair if you're going to ride my ass!" She handed some of the ammo to everyone. Next to them another Titan was cut in half by a laser beam and blew up. Calvin snapped, "No more standing around! Let's go!"

"Where, old man? We're getting fucking massacred!" Audie shouted at him in frustration as they came under fire. Calvin pointed to the mountain, "Get there, kill that bitch, and make the damned switch! Same as before! Fucking go!"

They deployed decoys and kept pushing forward going to the next thing that would count as concealment. There were several mortar rounds landing all around them along with plasma rounds. The Harpies were packed up around the roof tops and corners of the city buildings. They kept taking pot shots at them. Lydia got carried away and started firing everything she had at the buildings ahead of them. She managed to buy enough time for everyone to move up. Calvin shouted, "Get to some cover!"

"Right," she said as she ducked down. When she did, a mortar round landed right in front of her Titan. "Shit!"

It went off sending her machine flying backwards with multiple holes in it. Both Calvin and Audie both rushed to her aid with the others firing to provide cover. They pulled her Titan into a crater as they got shot at. They saw the cockpit took a lot of shrapnel. Lydia asked weakly, "Is it bad?"

"No. You'll be fine!" Audie said with grief in his voice. Lydia laughed, "You know I can tell when you're lying, right?"

"We've gotten out of worse than this! You just started to get good!" Calvin shouted at her as the rounds kept landing around them. "I'll do better next time... oh wait... never mind," she remembered that the Pandora had been shot down in a bleak acceptance of her fate. Several more mortar hits landed around them. Dirt, metal, and glass went up into the air and rained back on top of them. As they used their shields to block the incoming objects, Calvin shouted, "We need to go!" Audie laughed, "I'm not leaving her!"

"This is what we wanted, love. Don't regret any of it! Tell our kids I said hi," she told him with a rasp. A round landed right next to his Titan. Lydia shouted, "I love you, Audie. Pain in the ass!"

She pushed his Titan out of the way and hopped on the round and took the blast saving everyone else. Her machine went up in flames as the fires burned through the metal. Audie lost it and rocketed toward the Valkyrie's position. He single handed started assaulting the motor units that were dropping fire on them. Audie fired his massive handheld cannon at them, taking out whole teams of them when the rounds struck their ammunition dumps. All the nearby Consortium forces still actively converged on the team pushing towards the mountain. Despite having control of the air, the Valkyries were in a full state of retreat as the Titans charged after them relentlessly. From above came a Consortium destroyer still fighting it out. It managed to dump multiple torpedoes onto the mountain, knocking out its shielding. As it fell, all the Mechs started making their way towards the entrance to the complex below. The destroyer was then hit multiple times and knocked out of the sky. Its last act was to pave the way for the Titans to advance. The volley of torpedoes wiped out whole divisions of Harpies in a flash. There were still good and plenty of them in front and behind them. Several of the Marine Titans started to turn their cannons around to hold off the incoming tide of enemy machines. Lane joined them as she grabbed an extra cannon and fired away with everything she had. "I'll hold these fuckers off as long as I can with the ground pounders! Get to the entrance!"

"You can't be…" Calvin got cut off when several rounds landed near him. He was forced to fly away from her. Her Titan gave him a nod as she held the line with the rest of the other Mechs. The rest of the team rushed forward across the no man's land, shooting at anything that moved in front of them. Audie was on a rampage, firing off his massive cannon repeatedly and leading the way. Then from above there was another massive explosion sending an avalanche of rock, snow and dirt down towards them. Calvin shouted, "No turning back. Either get in the mountain or get crushed!"

All the Titans moved forward towards the entrance, pushing their boosters to the limit. The gate in front of them had multiple Harpies in the way. Audie rushed ahead, cutting four of them in half in one swoop of his sabers. He fired his chest and torso mounted cannons downing another two of them. The doors started to close on top of him. He used his Mech to hold it open. All the other Titans rushed past him using the opportunity to get inside. Calvin stopped at the door to provide cover for the others to enter. He laughed, "Good job kid!"

"Thanks. That's the first compliment that I think you…" Audie got cut off when his machine was hit right in the cockpit. His machine managed to hold the door open just a bit longer as the mountain rocked with the landslide about to hit. Not all the Titans were going to make it. Calvin kicked the destroyed machine out of the way allowing the door to slam shut just as rocks from the avalanche impacted in front of him leaving him in the dark.

CHAPTER 22
STANDING FOR SOMETHING
2276
VALHALLA
MOUNTAIN BRUNHILDE
ENTRANCE

CALVIN adjusted his vision as the area was clear. He was amazed at how large the structure was. It could house hundreds of Mechs. It looked like the bay was meant to be a landing area for transports, like an airline terminal. The walls were covered in mirrors displaying static information in a different language. The Titans that made it in made quick work of the drones and auto turrets inside. Barbra laughed as she smashed one of the turrets, "Shell might have been thick, but the inside is weak as hell!"

Calvin did a quick count and saw that only forty other Titans made it inside. Seeing this drove home how badly their forces had been whittled down. He looked at the door knowing that it was all that was standing between them and death. Barbra moved up to him and commented, "Well this certainly sucks for them."

Valery scoffed, "Feels more like a blowing analogy to me."

The doors leading to the outside started to rock. Hail gasped knowing what was on the other side, "Shit. Looks like we're going to have to kill them all by ourselves."

"Good. Plenty for each of us to kill," Calvin started

laughing. Once more he was being sent in to topple an empire while being thrown to the wolves. This was his choice after all. Lane came over the comms, "They're going to start breaking back in soon. We're getting decimated. Been a hell of a…"

The signal went dead. He sighed, accepting his situation and fate, "Everyone listen up."

All the other Titans looked towards him giving him their attention as the doors rocked again with dust coming down from above. Calvin ordered, "Hail and Barbra. Take eighteen Marines and storm inside. Kill that bitch."

"Cal, where's the person we're supposed to put in her place?" Valery asked him when he realized he didn't know. He laughed, "We'll worry about that after we kill her counterpart. Will you hold the line with me and the eighteen Marines?"

"We're in it to the end," she told him as the mountain rocked from the Valkyrie forces starting to dig their way in. Helena scoffed, "You have lost your mind."

Calvin smiled as he looked at the doors as they were hit again. He took off his helmet, threw it inside in the cockpit and loosened up the collar around his neck. "Yep. It's going to be magnificent."

Hail's Titan came up to his and grabbed his shoulder, "Dad, we have enough dead heroes! We can just blow up the doors as we go along, cause a cave in or two, set up traps… anything else besides leaving you behind!"

"Son, none of us were going to get off this rock alive. We are going to go out swinging. We'll give you all enough time to accomplish the mission," Calvin told him as the doors rocked once more with the edges buckling. Barbra snapped at him, "I'm sorry about your friends, but we need you with us, not as a doorstop!"

Hail tried one more time to change his mind, "Dad, come with us for crying out loud. Don't do this!"

"The order has been given! You're wasting time. If you get to the afterlife first, tell Yeager 'No hard feelings' for me, will you?" Calvin told him. Hail sighed, "Will do. See you at the victory party."

"Right. Marines, have the automated Mechs be the first line. We'll hold back and pick them off for as long as they stand. Don't be finicky with ammo. When you run dry or get damaged, send your Titan on a kamikaze and pull back. Understood?"

"Hoorah!" They shouted as they followed the orders. Each of them scrambled to make cover where they could, set up mines, and set up kill zones. Barbra sighed, "Been fun for what time we had."

"Fun isn't over yet. Go," he told her. Hail gave him a salute as he led Barbra and eighteen of the Marines after setting their Mechs to autopilot. They rushed over to the small doors to breach them. In a loud bang, they stormed inside. Calvin and the remaining manned Mechs started preparing as best they could so they'd be ready for the fight to come. Valery sighed, "I think chilling out while high on a frozen roof top would have been just as good."

"Would it have been glorious?" Calvin asked her as the mountain rocked once more. Valery laughed, "Good point. Let's be offensive. I know what I said!"

Light started to shine through from the outside as the entrance was about to be breached. Calvin felt a tear going down his face and quickly wiped it away. Helena told him, "That was touching. So how long do you think you'll be able to hold them before fleeing?"

"Prefer the term tactical withdrawal. Maybe five minutes," Calvin told her jokingly. In the few minutes they had left, they deployed ever decoy they had left in front of the machines and used what fragments he could find to create cover for the Titans. The automated ones sped up his preparations as they joined in his work effort. Calvin had the Titans line up in four to defend groups of ten. His Titan was at the end with multiple weapons around him. He had it where once one line would fall, the machines could pull back to another while having cover fire. He aimed the sights of his rifle downrange towards the doors as they bucked again with more light shining through. Valery sighed, "The end is here."

"Let's make it a good one. Marines, let's give them hell!" Calvin shouted as they aimed their weapons, ready to fire. Helena sighed, "Why did you have to be so noble?"

"Not nobility. Like I said, I wanted to go out with my boots on instead of getting shot in a straitjacket. Now kindly shut up!" He told her as the doors bent. It would only be one more push before they'd come down. Calvin already had an escape route in mind for when his Titan got shot down. He would hold off on ejecting until the last moment. His machine stayed knelt with the large cannon held steady. Helena sighed, "Fine. With you to the end. I don't have a choice in the matter."

"Yes, you do," he told her as the doors few open. Calvin quickly pulled back on the trigger and fired. With one shot he halved thirty machines in front of him with a long, concentrated blast of his laser cannon. The heat from the weapon turned the bay into an oven with everything becoming heated. The Valkyrie machines all scrambled to get out of the way. He took another shot, downing another ten Harpies. He threw aside the burnt-out cannon and grabbed another one. The Valkyries responded by sending a wave of explosives into the bay. All the automated Titans ducked behind the cover as they went off. Calvin returned the favor by firing off multiple proximity rounds. The blast rocked the mountain as they went off. He couldn't tell how many he took down in the volley. After a click, he threw the empty cannon aside and made another switch. Valery laughed, "Beats reloading!"

"Hell yeah!"

The opening got ripped open wider with a wave of Harpies charging in. The automated Titans popped up from their cover and opened fire. The enemy Mechs seemed to be caught by surprise as the first wave of them was cut down. Calvin got the next weapon ready as the first rank ducked down to reload. The second one opened fire, chewing up more drones. Once the ranks switched out, the Harpies joined together to form a shield and moved their way into the bay. Calvin shouted, "First rank, pull back!"

The unmanned machines moved back while getting cover from the second row. They left behind mines for the Harpies to walk on top of. The blast broke the shield and left the machines exposed. The storm of rounds went right through them. The machines burst open and toppled over onto their fallen counterparts. The bay was starting to get filled with smoke from the burning wrecks pilling up on the floor. Despite the losses, the Valkyries now had a foot hold in the bay. They moved in and started picking off the unmanned Titans. Five of them went down in quick succession as they took hits right to the torso. Calvin joined back in firing a laser cannon, cutting a dozen machines in half. Before he could fire again, the weapon was shot out of his mechanical arms. He gasped, "Shit!"

The Harpies rushed forward, destroying the first line of Titans. Valery held them off with her own cannon sawing another dozen in half with a sweep of the muzzle. The second line was able to pull back with only the third covering them. Calvin fired away with two handheld cannons at once downing five more enemy machines. Aiming wasn't needed as the Valkyries were at point blank range. Despite this, they managed to go through multiple explosives. The three unmanned Titans took the hits for him and shielded the man machines from the blast. "Third rank pull back. Fourth, cover!"

As the fragments of the destroyed Mechs of the second line flew back at him, Helena sighed, "Thought this would last longer."

"Not over yet!" he shouted at her as he had his Titan empty its ammunition. He just swept side to side. The other machines in the line did the same. "Fourth line pull back! Third, cover!"

They moved further back into the bay as the next line covered their retreat. They got to the next set of cover and joined in the shooting gallery. The Harpies once more banded together and were making progress towards them. They even managed to shoot down two manned Mechs. Seeing as the enemy was picking up its pace Calvin shouted, "Charge!"

The eighteen remaining Titans boost forward while blasting away with what ammo they had left. Once they got close, they pulled their sabers out engaging in melee. He stabbed two machines in the torso while blasting apart another with his torso mount weapons. Valery hacked four in half with a swipe of her blades. The Marines were also getting their stabbing in as they pushed the Harpies back once more. Calvin spun around, dodging the plasma rounds, and cut another two in half. The Harpies pulled back and fired at them. Four more Titans were cut down in the onslaught. One of them managed to do a suicide attack taking down three Harpies with him. "Pull back!"

Calvin blocked the rounds with his shield and grabbed another cannon and fired back. Two more Titans fell as they got back into cover and pulled out saved weapons to fight back with. As they were emptying their magazines, Valery pointed out, "We're not going to be able to hold off another wave!"

"Time to sacrifice the machines then." Calvin knew that soon his machine would get shot down from under him and started pulling back to the doors that were just breached, "Egress!"

The remaining twelve Mech leapt back into the bay, getting ready to bail out. Despite throwing as much ordnance downrange as he could, the Valkyries rushed forward. Calvin sighed with regret as he discreetly abandoned his machine, "Ditch!"

Calvin and the eleven others rushed toward the ruptured doors. Their Titans held on a bit longer. Each one went down fighting. When they ran out of ammo, they used their sabers. When their stabbers broke, they used knives. When those were lost, they used their bare hands. One by one the giants fell. As the last Titan slowly died, it fired off the last of its ammo, taking down two more Mechs. Calvin, Valery, and eight others made it into the complex. The debris killed two Marine pilots. He saw multiple mines that stayed dormant as he made his way into a passageway that had mirrors on all four sides. There were signs of a fight with bullet holes all over and burn marks. Thankfully, no downed Marines or family members. Helena told him, "You should have kept your helmet on."

Calvin shouted, "We're in it to win it! Marines activate the booby traps and move back to the kill points. Let's make them bleed!"

"Hoorah!"

"Hoo-fucking-rah."

CHAPTER 23
PUNCHING BAG
2276
VALHALLA
MOUNTAIN BRUNHILDE
PASSAGEWAY

CALVIN aimed down the passageway from a corner. He fired off multiple guided rounds that twisted, turned, and flew into the incoming drones crowded around the entrance. He laughed as they were destroyed by the dozen. Once he ran out of ammo, he pulled back to the next point allowing the Valkyrie forces to follow him into the death traps. He ducked down as the Marines shot apart the drones chasing after them, forcing them back. Once he passed them, they activated a turret to shoot anything that came after them. Valery was right next to him, "Cutting it close?"

Calvin huffed, "We're still ten strong and haven't seen any breacher casualties yet. We're doing something right!"

The turret went silent after being overrun. The mines behind him made the hallway vibrate with every blast that went off. He stayed on his feet, making it to the next check point, grabbed another rocket launcher and fired another salvo. This time however, the missiles went off prematurely. Valkyrie pulled him down as the shrapnel came flying at them. A Marine fell, beheaded by one of the fragments. "Fuck!"

"I'll say," Valery stabbed herself with a syringe to

keep herself from bleeding out. Helena told him, "They're catching up."

"Wouldn't be fun if they didn't," he told her, pulling back again. Valery and Calvin took turns covering one other as the Marines kept setting up more traps to be activated. Calvin looked over, "You alright?"

"Fine. Just keep fighting!" The mines stopped going off once more. One of the Marines shouted, "We're out of mines and traps, going to have to shoot them the old-fashioned way."

Calvin sighed, "Fight in groups of two, empty your mags and pull back with the next group covering!"

He knew that the real fight was about to begin as their traps were all being sprung. He started collecting weapons as he went along. Once he had a cannon with shrapnel rounds in it, he spun around as heavily armored drones rounded the corner. He held down the trigger, sending a wave of multinet plasma at them. Each recoil sent him back a few feet with a deafening bang snapping through the air. The machines kept moving forward despite being ripped to shreds. The weapon overheated, and he threw it like a javelin into a machine, making it blow up. Valery covered him as he switched weapons shooting down six more machines. "Fucking cowards! Fight yourselves instead of using fucking bots!"

Valery ran and Calvin pulled a machine gun and fired again. It disturbed him that the machines weren't firing back. They were just taking the rounds like metal shields. No matter how many he shot down, more took their place. They increased their pace, getting closer to him. He ran backwards while keeping up the fire. Valery stayed by his side slowly moving back. A Marine shouted, "Duck!"

They did so as a shotgun blast decimated the robots. "Go! I'll hold them!"

Both nodded and went into a full sprint. Once the shooting stopped, Valery and Calvin dropped all the grenades they had left for the machines to run into. As they retreated, they started finding members of the breacher team dead among the machines and Valkyrie fighters. Valery sighed, "We're reaching the…"

"Fun part. Lighten up," he told her as she nodded in agreement. Everything was quiet. He didn't hear the stomping of their metal feet or anything else. Calvin pulled a shotgun out and aimed it down the passageway waiting. A Marine got on the comms, "We've caught up to the breacher team. There's only twelve of us left."

"Join them and push ahead. Valery and I will hold them for as long as we can. Get some!"

"Fuck yeah!"

"Here they come," Valery told him as Calvin threw his only decoy to the other side of the hull. The lights started flashing around him to confuse his vision. He grunted, "Come and get us bitches!"

"You're going to die!" Valery shouted.

"You're dead," Helena told him mockingly as two soldiers in silver clad armored suits came towards them. They were almost as tall as he was. They both had weapons mounted all over the suit and plasma swords on their backs. They quickly fired at them. The two dodged the rounds and managed to close the distance in an instant. They used the shotgun as a shield as they stabbed at them. Both blocked the strikes while being pushed back. Calvin tried kicking one of them, but they leaned back and pulled his leg, making him flip upside down then, and then kicked him in the back sending him flying down the passageway and into a wall. Valery was alone dodging the strikes. She pulled out two knives and managed to stab one of them in the thigh. Her hand got chopped off in the process. She moved back blocking another strike with the stump arm losing more of the limb. Calvin was back in the fight stabbing one of them in the torso with both his knives and kicking it backwards. Valery was headbutted and fell backwards. Calvin started getting pummeled by the enraged operative. They focused on his torso, denting in his armor. Helena shouted at him, "Use the fucking last resort you moron!"

"Deus Ex Machina," he thought aloud, realizing he didn't have to hold back. Calvin blocked the next set of punches and snapped both her arms. Before she could pull back, he grabbed his knives and stabbed her in the neck, killing them. The drones opened fire on him as he leaped forward stabbing the machines right in their reactor. He quickly holstered the knives, grabbed a cannon, and halved all the machines in the passageway. Four more operators came at him. Two got shot down and Valery attached a shotgun to her stump and used the other arm to fire the weapon. Calvin used this to close the distance with the other two. With his plasma pistols he stabbed them both in the neck. After they dropped, he moved back. "Come on."

Valery followed covering his six as they started coming across fallen Marines and dead Valkyrie operatives. Out of necessity, he used the armor from the fallen to quickly repair his suit, get extra ammo, and found a couple more grenades. He shared them with Valery, as she was hurting from the hits she took. "Fuckers are going to pay for shooting me!"

"Yes, they are. Hang in there." He told her as she nodded in agreement. "Take my helmet off. It's not functioning."

He obliged and pushed her hair back out of her face. "We got this."

"Hell yeah."

They managed to get the finishing touches in as the drones and operators caught up to them. The drones soaked up the rounds while the soldiers closed the distance. Calvin laughed, "Taking this ass kicking personal?"

Again, they clashed, a blade with a loud echoing snap slicing the air. Calvin at first just blocked the strikes before going back on the offensive. He chopped the head off one of them and stabbed another one in its face mask.

With a kick, he sent another operator flying back and into the wall. Calvin blocked a lunge from the fourth operator and fired off the shotguns mounted to his leg, sending her flat on the deck missing her arms. Her helmet came off showing her face. He looked down at her stunned by her physical features. Despite being an alien, she was easy on the eyes to him. Valery shot her in the face and then shot eight drones and two operatives in quick succession. "You're getting in the way!"

"Don't be a spoiled sport!"

He looked back up, seeing the other operative taking a shot at him.

Calvin moved back and retreated. Valery ditched the shotgun and used one of the plasma sabers. Helena snapped at them, "Keep your damned heads in the game!"

"What does it look like we're doing?" He looked over at her.

Valery shouted, "Duck!"

Calvin did so as they came under fire from a group of operatives that came charging at their front. One of them stomped on Calvin's chest and was about to shoot him in the head. The saber impaled her neck, dropping her to the deck. Valery gasped weakly "Cal…"

Calvin stood up seeing Valery falling to the deck with multiple wounds on her torso and half her face burnt. "No, no, no!"

A wave of rounds came at him. He used an energy shield to deflect them all while pulling Valery back. "Cal… I'm done. Go."

"We end this together!" He shouted at her as his shields were going down. She activated a grenade and gasped, "Go love!"

With tears in his eyes, he moved back as fast as he could letting the operatives shoot Valery down. When they passed her body, the grenade went off in the air killing six of them. Calvin's blood boiled and he saw red once more. Holding nothing back, he charged ahead. He swung his

163

plasma knives upwards cutting right through the armor and through the skin. Calvin ducked down avoiding getting shot. He pulled his pistols out and shot the two operators repeatedly. After downing them, he broke out of his berserker state when a flame thrower forced him back. Calvin went as fast as he could down the passageway. He suddenly skidded to a stop when he saw Barbra bleeding out. "They need help."

She gestured with a grenade for him to go on. Calvin nodded to her as he ran. He made good distance before the grenade went off. He put aside his grief and focused on pure rage to push ahead. He came upon a massive throne like room with their target sitting calmly in a chair at the very end of the brightly lit room. The banners were on fire. The floor was littered with the fallen. Hail and two Marines were fighting their way to her. Calvin joined the fight by attacking the reinforcements coming at their side. When his pistols ran dry, he went back to the knives rapidly stabbing multiple drones and operatives in quick succession. He ended up with his back next to Hail as the last two Marines fell to their wounds. "Just us now son!"

"Can you give me an opening?" He asked as he looked over to Sophia and the remaining eight guards charging them. More operatives and drones followed them into the larger room. "Go for the bitch! I'll hold the rest!"

He vertically cut two drones in half and then stabbed two operatives in their head. Calvin moved back, dodging the strikes. He moved forward, cutting another two machines in half, and moved back, dodging multiple rounds. Then Calvin went forward and chopped another operative's head off. He ducked down from two stabber strikes and stabbed the operatives in their eyes. His right arm suddenly got chopped off. He quickly cauterized the wound, leaving a burnt stump. He rocked backward firing away with his pistol, desperately holding off the remaining horde. The drones took the hits as the operatives closed in around him. He passed over more fallen Marines and Valkyries alike. While Hail was dealing with now four Guards, Calvin was on the defensive, being pushed back and taking wound from lucky shots. Calvin dropped down avoiding being hit once more. Calvin ripped off one of the arms of the fallen and stuck it on his own body. It melded together allowing him to use the limb. Then he pulled up two plasma sabers and made a stand. He suddenly blocked a plasma saber being thrown from an operator in a golden suit. She pulled off her helmet showing her long white hair, pale skin, pointed nose, thin face, and wide blue eyes. The others stood by behind her as she started to walk forward letting her helmet drop. He smiled at her, "Thought you snobs were too good to do your own dirty work."

"Thought you apes were too dumb to fight back. Guess we both underestimated each other, primitive," she told him just before lunging at him with her saber. He blocked the strike and elbowed her in the face. She kicked him in the back of the knee and tried to cut his head off. Calvin leaned back and punched her in the torso, sending her back. He was suddenly shot multiple times. His armor bucked from the hits, his boosters went offline, and his shields were fried. He fired back, shooting the operators. Yet, one round hit him right in the head taking away his right eye. The lead operative came back at him swinging her saber. He blocked the attack, stuck a knife into her torso, and kicked it in deeper. She kicked him up into the ceiling and then head butted him onto his back. He bent his legs back and fired his mounted shotguns one more time. Her armored suit was ripped apart, but she was still in the fight. Calvin was suddenly stabbed multiple times over with plasma bayonets. He swung his sabers, cutting the arms off the soldiers and machines that attacked him and shooting them in the head to finish them off. Then the golden one stabbed him in the crotch. He let out a painful yelp as he returned the favor and stabbed in her in the same spot. Both shot each other with their side arms in the torso multiple times. Both then stabbed each other in the right hand then jabbed the blades into each other's necks. They were both still as they looked each other in the eyes. They shared an expression of agony as tears came from their eyes. Calvin then started laughing as he got stabbed again with multiple bayonets. He let go of the knife as the golden operative was pulled back to get medical attention. Calvin dropped to his knees. Everything became quiet. "Hail?"

He looked back only to see him fallen with the other four guards dead around him. Their target started clapping, "I'm impressed. You all made it farther than I thought. Had me worried there for a second that I might get a scratch. Fantastic job by the way." Then she turned to her crew, "You let a pack of mongrels give you a hard time."

The operatives scoffed at her. The golden warrior shouted in her language in protest. The short alien lifted a hand, and she was silent, "You apes couldn't have done this yourself. Who sent you?"

Calvin started laughing through the pain and agony he was in. "What's so funny mongrel?" asked the Sophia lookalike.

He couldn't talk. Calvin just pointed at her and mouthed the words, "You."

The alien looked puzzled for a second. Her look turned to pure terror when she realized what he was talking about. It was too late. Eight Mongol operatives suddenly surrounded Calvin. Before the Valkyries could react, they were all cut down in seconds in a quick burst of fire. The golden warrior was the last to fall as she almost got close to the Mongols. She was gasping on blood and scowling at Calvin. "Tough break bitch," he smirked.

She fell face first onto the deck while dying on the floor. Sophia came out from behind the Mongols. Her counterpart went from shocked to dismayed knowing her fate was sealed. "Figured I'd do myself in."

"Oh, the puns. You make me ashamed to be

166

myself," she told her as she huffed, "You're the one who had to use apes."

"You're the one that lost to them. Friends, end her life however you see fit," Sophia told them as one of them pulled out a flame thrower. "Fuck you!"

The Sophia double screamed in agony as she was bathed in flames. It lasted a solid minute before she was reduced to ash after a second spray of the flame thrower. Calvin gasped, "Showoffs."

He collapsed onto the floor from his wounds, landing on his side to last a bit longer. He laughed again, "It's cold here."

"Never took you for a bleeding heart," one of the Mongols told him. Calvin recognized the voice. "Yeager?"

"One of many."

Another of them pulled off their helmet showing their face, "Well done, you lunatic. I knew I could count on you."

"Helena?" Calvin gasped at seeing her. She nodded, "Bummer about Valery. I liked her. At least we have you."

Calvin couldn't speak as he was starting to fade. He then felt a jab that stopped his bleeding. Calvin gasped, "What?"

"Sorry. Today isn't your day to die," Doc's voice chirped from the armored suit. Calvin started to stand up when Murphy jabbed him again. Calvin collapsed to the floor on his back. "You played your part as well as you did before, and as you will again. So much fun."

"Sorry I wasn't more honest with you. I was leading you on," Holly told him showing her face.

Calvin realized what she meant. He struggled once more to stand. Another injection and he was back on the ground. Calvin tried lifting his arm but couldn't lift it up. Weakly he rasped, "Fuck you!"

"Ungrateful as always," Doc sighed. Calvin sighed, "Deus Ex Machina…"

"Different timelines, different rules. You're not pulling a …" Calvin leaped up punching Murphy in the face mask, breaking it and sending him onto his back with a broken nose. Calvin laughed, "Smug prick…"

He faceplanted on the deck unable to move. Doc removed his helmet and face mask. "Well, he's gotten stronger."

"You're getting too cocky, old man," Yeager told him.

"Well, the throne is yours, Sophia. Mind your end of the bargain, and so will we," Helena told her as she smiled, "A deal is a deal."

Doc walked up to Calvin sighing, "Goodbye, Calvin Marley."

EPILOGUE

A rubber glove forced a set of eye lids apart, letting in the surrounding light. It stung like burning needles being jabbed into his retinas. As he grunted trying to close his eyes and move, a cheerful voice said, "Patient is responding to stimuli. I was wondering when you'd wake up."

"I was having a good dream… I can't remember it though. Who are you?" the man asked, confused on where he was and what was going on. The Doctor nodded, "I see you can still communicate. Hope you didn't lose any other talents. You're going to need them."

"What do you mean? Could you stop being so vague. I feel like I just got done with a month-long bender." The man felt like his skull was going to crack. The Doctor explained, "You took some nasty head trauma. Seems that you have amnesia. What's the last thing you remember doing?"

"I was banging… I can't remember." He pulled back from the insult as this was lost. When he tried thinking of before that moment, all that came up was a blur. He looked around the infirmary seeing the normal medical equipment, beds and scanners around the room. "Shit… I can't remember… anything."

The man felt the Grey-haired Doctor yank out a cord from his belly, "A little warning?"

"Do you know why you are here?"

The man scoffed, "Rhetorical question don't you think?"

"You're right. Still feeling sore?" Doctor asked him. The man looked at a mirror seeing he was in green coveralls, black boots and brown shirt. He had pale skin, blonde hair and green eyes. "Sore. Yeah. This doesn't feel right."

"You'll get used to your augmentations. They saved your life after all. You're welcome," the Doctor smugly told him. The man sighed, "Seems you couldn't save my memory. I think that was kind of important."

"Not compared to muscle memory. There are going to be three people coming through that door to kill you in twenty seconds. Kill them, and you'll have a job. Don't and your body will be thrown out the airlock," the Doctor cut to the chase. The man looked at him with wide eyes, "What?"

"Fifteen seconds. You should get ready," the doctor told him as the man realized he wasn't joking. "What the fuck?"

"Ten seconds," he told him as he backed into a corner as the doors started to open, "Five, four, three, two..."

The doors were thrown open. Two men and a woman came charging at the man holding knives. Time slowed down for the man as he moved to the side, broke the first man's arm, stabbed him in the neck, ducked down dodging a stab, shoved the knife up the woman's nose, spun around the falling body and stabbed the last man in the back of the head. He let the body fall with the knife still impaled inside. He stood there for several seconds. "I feel like I've done this before."

Doc smiled, "What can I say? You're a natural born   killer."

www.ingramcontent.com/pod-product-compliance
Lightning Source LLC
Chambersburg PA
CBHW060647260626
47161CB00008B/3028